FROZEN GIRL OF SPIRIT LAKE

MEG LELVIS

Black Rose Writing | Texas

The author grants the final approval for this literary material.

First printing

This is a work of fiction. Names, characters, businesses, places, events, and incidents are either the products of the author's imagination or used in a fictitious manner. Any resemblance to actual persons, living or dead, or actual events is purely coincidental.

ISBN: 978-1-68513-415-0
PUBLISHED BY BLACK ROSE WRITING
www.blackrosewriting.com

Printed in the United States of America
Suggested Retail Price (SRP) $21.95

Frozen Girl of Spirit Lake is printed in Book Antiqua

*As a planet-friendly publisher, Black Rose Writing does its best to eliminate unnecessary waste to reduce paper usage and energy costs, while never compromising the reading experience. As a result, the final word count vs. page count may not meet common expectations.

In memory of my *father*, who wrote of Minnesota

&

In honor of my Minnesota cousins, *Myrna and Joel*

SPECIAL THANKS TO:

Reagan Rothe and his staff at Black Rose Writing
David King, Design Director at Black Rose Writing
Danielle Hartman Acee, Tech assistant
Mark Pople, Editor

Houston and Orlando critique partners:
Landy Reed, Linda Bycz, Mary Rosette, Katherine Vaccaro,
Jeanne Parks, and Bob Coombs

For advice and reminders of lakes, pines, walleyes, and all things
Minnesota: Carole, Ted, Myrna, and Gary

My family's continued support: Gary, Kristy, Rebecca, Cate,
Nolan, Theo, John, and Roni

FROZEN GIRL OF SPIRIT LAKE

The snow had begun in the gloaming,
And busily all the night
Had been heaping field and highway
With a silence deep and white.
–James Russell Lowell, *The First Snowfall*

There, in my dream,
I am one with my ancestors,
The only sound is the wind that moves the fluttering feathers.
–Ojibwe poem

THE TOWN AND ITS NEIGHBOR

1950s

On the surface, life was good in Eklund, Minnesota. In its post-war years, folks seemed untroubled, even carefree in their day-to-day lives. But small towns like Eklund harbor secrets. Secrets that lie dormant until they unexpectedly surface, ripping the social fabric of the entire community.

However, according to the local Chamber of Commerce, Eklund, Minnesota, was an idyllic place to live and raise a family. Located 100 miles south of the Canadian border, the picturesque town of 10,000 rested on the shores of Spirit Lake and housed one of five state colleges. Its fortunate residents enjoyed the beauty of nature with its change of seasons, outdoor winter and summer sports, and even a summer theater.

Eklund State Teachers College provided affordable higher education, along with a host of cultural events. Nestled among stately Norway pines framing Spirit Lake, its campus was considered the loveliest of the state colleges in Minnesota. But under this pleasant veneer lurked a rigid, ominous social hierarchy with unspoken rules. Some might call it a caste system, even in small-town Minnesota.

• • •

The Chamber's brochures gave no mention that Eklund was established in 1890, claiming its first permanent resident as an Ojibwe Indian chief of the tribe commonly called Chippewa. No one in town seemed to give much mind to the occasional Indian thrown in jail for drunk and disorderly conduct. Or the Indian kid who stole a bag of Dum-Dum pops from the local Ben Franklin. They only ventured into town on weekends, if at all.

About 40 miles northwest of Eklund, Thunder Lake Chippewa Reservation sprawled over 1,200 square miles of land, adorned by an extensive lake and scattered ponds. Although close in proximity to Eklund, the 2,700 reservation inhabitants remained decades behind in prosperity and comfort.

The Indians had their own worn-down schools with worn-down textbooks. A couple shabby corner grocery stores and shabbier bars sat forlornly along the grubby street waiting for better days.

Tribal law enforcement held sway and engaged in occasional scuffles with state or local cops if crimes crossed boundaries.

The highlight on the reservation was fishing on Thunder Lake, filled to the brim with Minnesota's quintessential fish: the walleyed pike. The Indians enjoyed full access to the most sought-after fish in the state, bending tribal restrictions of selling the treasured walleye to tourists along dusty roads.

Admittedly, most Chippewas minded their own business. They'd come to Eklund for banking and court cases, lingering by the door until everyone else was finished.

They lived on the outskirts of life. That is, until the winter of 1955.

CHAPTER 1

Nancy
Saturday, February 19, 1955

The day began like any other in my icy corner of the world. Even for northern Minnesota, the winter had been brutal. Old-timers claimed it hadn't been this cold in a coon's age. January lasted for months in both directions.

That Saturday morning in February, another frigid day awaited us winter-weary folks of Eklund. The cold prowled in every corner and preyed on skin and bones, slipping with ease through layers of wool shrouding anyone who braved the outdoors. Then the wind, as if it felt neglected, lashed its way across sidewalks and yards, sculpting snow into peaks and swirls like giant Dairy Queen cones. Yes, the arctic spell tried our patience as Jack Frost made his customary yearly visit and decided to stay for weeks on end.

Struggling into my bulky red parka, I braced myself for the bitter onslaught, numbly resigned to my fate as I reached for the front door knob. The freezing weather was annoying as hell and altogether miserable. Warnings drummed into us since birth echoed in my mind: drive slowly with no less than a half tank of gas, always have blankets, a bag of sand or kitty litter, and a flashlight in your trunk. Last year, a med student crashed into a telephone pole while driving too fast on ice-slicked County Road

D and ended up a paraplegic. A grim reminder of what can happen if you're not careful. But winter was not a danger to someone like me. Not really.

I pondered my final months of college before escaping this one-horse town to job-hunt in California. Next quarter I would student teach and finally graduate in June. Then at last, I'd break free of Eklund and my father.

"Nancy, wait a minute," my mother called from the kitchen. "I just heard on the radio—"

Oh crap, no time for her weather report. Snow or not, I was determined to leave and meet my friend after a grueling week of midterm exams and my father's worse-than-usual temperament.

Mom hurried into the living room, breathless. "Oh, Nancy, some poor college girl was found frozen to death in a snowbank this morning!"

My heart skipped a beat. "Oh my God, who was she? What happened to—"

"They're not saying her name." Mom wiped her hands on her flowered apron. "It seems she left a party last night and tried to walk back to her dorm. I can't imagine why anyone would go out in a blizzard alone."

I didn't want to tell my mother the girl may have been drunk and wandered off. Mom thought college was safe, which it was. Well, usually.

"Terrible news, Mom. I'm on my way to meet Peggy. Maybe she's heard something. Keep the radio on. Big news for this little burg."

"It's twenty below and snowing. It'll get worse. Look what just happened. You'll need—"

"Mother, please. I'm a senior in college." I opened the door and stomped out before she could protest further.

The wind sank its fangs into my cheeks as I gingerly navigated the sidewalk, shuffling in my boots so I wouldn't slip. I'd forgotten to take my Bayer this morning, so I'd have to cope with the inevitable backache that cold weather inflicted on my spinal condition. I'd ask Peggy for aspirin.

A blanket of white smothered the city, with swirling feathery flakes nearly blinding me as I trudged along 14th Street toward Peggy's apartment. Hugging myself against the bitter gusts, head down, I contemplated the identity of the poor frozen girl. Did I know her?

Nothing this tragic ever happened in Eklund except back in the 1920s when little Sally Roy had frozen in a blizzard on winter solstice. The six-year-old had snuck outdoors while her mother baked cookies, thinking the girl was playing in her room. Since then, parents and teachers repeated the tale, drilling their children not go outdoors alone in a snowstorm. I can still see Miss Hoganson's wrinkled cheeks and downturned mouth as she told my first-grade class the story. Local folklore claimed that the specter of Sally Roy, captured by Chippewa Indians, still haunts the shores of Spirit Lake every year. But winter solstice was two months ago. Besides, I scoffed at the notion of ghosts.

I looked up as wind whipped my face. Shocked, I nearly collided with a bear-sized man all in black, carrying a small grocery bag. He pulled his long scarf from his face.

"Good Lord, Roland, what are you doing out here?" Roland Nightbird stood stiff, piercing me with black, endless eyes. I wondered why on earth he was in town. Didn't he stay with his family at Thunder Lake reservation on weekends?

He cleared his throat. "Roads too bad to drive home last night. Stayed with my uncle."

I nodded, shivering. "Say, did you hear about … oh, nothing. Well, better get on. I'm almost at my friend's place."

"Hear about what?"

Suddenly uncomfortable, I muttered, "Um, just more snow, blizzard's getting—"

"Yeah, I know." His muffled voice disappeared in the wind.

Eager to seek warmth at Peggy's, I tightened my hood. "Well, be careful. See ya."

He raised his ham-sized mittened paw in a wave, turning, soon invisible in a blank canvas of snowdrifts.

I reached Peggy Olsen's upstairs apartment in a large stone house near Spirit Lake. Marshmallow puffs of snow latched onto empty branches of birches and spruce trees. Icicles hung in uneven rows along the portico, like translucent fingers pointing to the slippery ground as if warning me. *Beware. Watch your step.* I rang Peggy's bell, stepped into the entryway, and plodded up the stairs. Outside her door, I yanked off my boots, left them dripping in the hallway, and shrugged out of my parka.

The door opened, and Peggy nearly dragged me toward her small kitchen.

"Come in, get warm. You're probably the only person crazy enough to be outside today."

"Not quite." I smelled coffee and cinnamon in the air. "I ran into Roland Nightbird on the way here. The guy looked frozen stiff."

"Really?" Peg's flaxen hair curtained her bony face. "What's he doing off the reservation on a Saturday?"

"The blizzard was too bad to drive yesterday, much less out in the boonies." I sighed. "Poor Roland. Bad enough being poor, plus an Indian to boot. I hope he never gets wind of the jerks who refer to him as 'Injun Joe.'"

Fortunately, Roland had landed a job working maintenance at the college, thanks to a man at the BIA, the federal Bureau of Indian Affairs.

I touched Peg's shoulder. "Oh my God, did you hear about the college girl they found this morning dead in a snowbank?" I pulled out a kitchen chair, and we sat at a Formica table with mugs of coffee and a plate of hot cinnamon buns. I warmed my hands, circling them around my cup and helped myself to a roll.

Her blue eyes widened. "Yeah, the poor frozen girl. My boss called earlier." Peggy was an admissions secretary at the college and was saving money to enroll as a student next fall. "The boss phoned everyone in admissions, but they're not releasing the girl's name. The girl left a party at a rental house on Elmcrest Drive, but her body was found on seventeenth near Northlake."

I took a few seconds to visualize the location. "Jeez, that's a long way from the dorm, especially walking in a blizzard. Good Lord. Freezing to death. I wonder if you suffer. Who found her?"

"Don't know." Peggy tapped two Winstons from a pack and offered me one. "Could be similar to drowning. I'll bet the boss knows her name, but she's sworn to secrecy for now." She lit our cigarettes and placed a tin ashtray on the table.

We were a threesome, best chums since kindergarten, my entire circle of friends. Judy Sandberg and I lived in town, students at Eklund College. Peggy couldn't afford to attend after graduation and needed to work. It turned out growing up poor was not her worst hardship. But I learned that later. Judy was the lucky one. At least so far.

Peggy and I prattled on about the frozen mystery girl until the telephone jangled in the living room. Anxious the call would bring more news, I followed Peggy as she dashed to pick up. She grabbed the black receiver. "Hello. Oh, hi Judy."

I waited, jiggling my foot.

"Oh my God. Oh no." I hovered around Peggy's shoulder, trying to listen.

After a minute of gasping out words of shock, she finally hung up. I nearly tripped over her as we returned to the kitchen.

Judy lived several blocks north of me. Her father, Dr. Will Sandberg, a long-time history professor, must've heard more details already.

Peggy's face remained pale as we fell into our chairs. Before she spoke, she took two deep breaths. "Oh God." Her words came out in chokes. "Can you believe, the poor girl was Barbara

Gruen. Yes, Dave's sister." Her hands trembled as she lit another cigarette. Dave was Judy's fiancé, so he was a close friend.

My heart drum-rolled across my chest. "What? His little sister? Barbara? Are they sure? I can't believe—"

Peggy held up her hands. "I know. Dave's in a frenzy. His parents are on their way from Grand Rapids."

"Lord, she was only a sophomore with her whole life ahead. Barbara was such a sweetie when she'd tag along with us." I lit my second cigarette with wobbly fingers. I needed to cut down, but now wasn't the time. "How did it happen?"

Peggy took a puff. "Barbara and two girlfriends had gone to a party across Northland Avenue at a rental house. Judy didn't know who lived there, or why Barbara showed up. Lots of beer, but they don't know if Barbara was drunk. Dave claimed she didn't drink. Anyway, she left the party alone they think. Must've lost her way in the blizzard."

I thought a second. "Yeah, Barbara sure doesn't … didn't seem like the type to drink much. She was so nice and quiet." I snuffed out my cigarette.

Peggy stood, shoestring thin, face ashen. "Think I should call my boss? Now that we know Barbara's name, maybe I'll hear more."

"Yes, call her. Find out who found her body. The cops? A neighbor?"

I felt sick. I visualized Barbara's heart-shaped face and pink mouth like a dab of cotton candy. No one close to me had died so young. How could that have happened to innocent little Barbara Gruen?

And why, out of nowhere, did the image of Roland Nightbird lurk in the shadows of my mind?

CHAPTER 2

Roland
Saturday

Saturday morning while the whole town griped about the worst winter in donkey's years, Roland Nightbird's mind was on other things. He trudged along 14th Street toward campus where he worked Saturdays in bad weather. He must not think about last night.

Because of the blizzard, he'd stayed the night with his Uncle Moose, who lived several miles from town on Spirit Lake. Moose's dumpy two-room cabin, painted bright aqua, sat among a group of similar huts in various stages of disrepair. At least the place was warmer than Roland's shack on the reservation.

Moose fished year around and eked out a living running a ramshackle bait shop where he sold minnows, leeches, worms, spinners, and stale Clark bars. He also kept a cooler of beer and pop for thirsty fishermen and rented out a couple of beat-up wooden row boats in the summer. The bait shop was on the lakeshore, buried in snow, waiting to resurrect itself with the advent of summer.

As Roland ambled along the slippery sidewalk this Saturday morning, he forced his mind to wander. He thought of his family, visualizing his father, George Nightbird, stoking up the wood stove in hopes of keeping the shack warm enough to survive another night not fit for Eskimos.

•   •   •

A gust of wind blew Roland back to the present as he pulled his scarf over his mouth and shuffled along. He passed well-kept two-story white and tan houses, a far cry from his shanty, as he called his dilapidated home at Thunder Lake. He lived in a former tarpaper shack with his father, George, Grandma Dinah, and two younger sisters. Last year they finally got running water through a small pump in the kitchen, but still no indoor toilet. Instead, they were stuck with the outhouse, thankfully promoted to a two-seater last summer after neighborly help from George's cronies.

Just keep goin', kid. You're twenty-four now. George's words stuck in Roland's head. *Take some college an' work hard. Got a lucky break gettin' that job an' stayin' with Moose.*

Yes, Roland knew he had to get out. Even if he was better off than most Indian kids, his grandmother's words last week disturbed him. *Some kids are being sent away. Nobody knows where. Men in suits come and get 'em. Somethin' to do with gettin' better care and wanting 'em to live like the white man and forget our way of life.*

She must've noticed Roland's look of fear. *Don't worry, kiddo, your ma ran off, but me and your pa take good care of you kids. Besides, you're too old.*

Roland rarely thought of his mother, who disappeared after the last baby, but Grandma Dinah moved in and took over the family like most grandmas would. Once in a blue moon, his father would come home drunk and start wobbling around, slurring words, sending chairs crashing to the floor.

Bitch running off God knows where. Leaving me stuck with kids, cookin'. Bitch. Gonna find her some day and pow —

Roland didn't take his dad's rantings seriously. After all, most of his pals had worse, like parents who were drunk all day or on drugs or beat the kids. Some lived with friends or relatives, or ended up in the system.

• • •

Two blocks from campus, something knocked him back to earth as he nearly collided with a red figure, hood pulled over a down-turned head.

"Good God, Roland, what are you doing out here?"

He cleared his throat. "Roads too bad to drive home last night." He recognized Nancy Borg, probably on her way to a friend's place. She tightened her gray knit scarf around her chin, her face as chapped and crimson as her jacket.

She and her friends always greeted him, unlike most of the stuck-up college girls. Nancy always treated him with kindness and sympathy. Someday she wouldn't see him as a poor Indian when he made it in this world.

Nancy shivered, then paused. "Say, did you hear about … oh, nothing. Well, better get on. I'm almost at Peggy's place."

"Hear about what?"

She coughed "Um, just more snow, blizzard's getting—"

"Yeah, I know." For a second he thought she'd ask about the girl who froze to death during the night. He was relieved Nancy didn't bring it up, but his gut said she may be hiding something. He gripped his grocery bag before it flew away.

With the wind lashing their faces, they went their separate ways. "Be careful, Roland. See ya."

Roland nodded and gave a half-wave. He just wanted to get warm and forget about what he'd seen last night.

CHAPTER 3

Nancy
Saturday

I squirmed in my chair while Peggy spoke to her boss. When they finally hung up, I blurted, "Well, what did the boss say? Who discovered the body … oops, I mean Barbara?"

"Just a sec. I need a beer." Peggy headed for the kitchen.

She took two cans of Hamm's from the fridge and busied herself at the counter making baloney and cheese sandwiches. Her hands quivered.

She began telling me the details. "Turns out, early this morning a neighbor lady took her dog out, and it was sniffing around a snowbank by the street. The lady about had a heart attack when she came closer and saw Barbara lying there. Called the cops." Peggy wiped crumbs from the table and continued talking.

"I don't know how they discovered where the party was, but Barbara went there with two girlfriends. One of them knew the guys who rented the apartment. Guess the landlord was away, and things got pretty wild. Later this morning, the cops questioned the guys, other guests, and Barbara's friends. All said the same thing." Peggy took a bite of her sandwich.

I leaned forward. "What? What did everybody say?"

Peggy held up her hand, chewing her food. She finally swallowed. "The boss said kids were drinking, dancing to loud music, pairing off. The friends noticed Barbara talked to this one guy, didn't know his name. Then she disappeared."

"The two girls kept apologizing to the cops," Peggy went on. "Said they'd talked Barbara into coming to the party, and she'd finally given in. Kept saying they should've kept track of her. When the girls got ready to go, they couldn't find Barbara and figured she'd left with the guy she'd talked to. But nobody saw her leave."

I shook my head. "I thought they were her friends."

"Really, Nancy, how were they supposed to know what would happen? I'm sure they'll feel guilty forever."

"Yeah, hate to admit it, but in hindsight, it could've happened to us I suppose." But secretly, I told myself I wouldn't have abandoned my friend, much less let her leave a party alone in a blizzard. Besides, it didn't sound like Barbara was the type who'd leave with a guy.

The story depleted me. I pictured an innocent girl, an outsider, trying to blend in and have fun. I knew the feeling, only too well.

I'd heard enough. Besides, my lousy back was killing me. I took a gulp of beer that tasted like warm pee. Not that I'd know the taste, but the image stuck in my mind.

"You look kind of sick." Peggy stared at me.

"I forgot my backache pills. Need aspirin for this damn headache too. Can we open a window?"

"In this weather? You must be sick." But she rose, unlocked a living room window, and grunted as she pushed it upward. "Crap, now snow's coming in."

I hurried over, bent down, and stuck my nose out the opening into a burst of gusty air, snowflakes settling on my nose and cheeks. I inhaled the freshness, a welcome relief from the stifling, smoky living room. "Ah, much better." I stood and pushed the window down with the edge of my palm.

"I'll get some aspirin for you." Peggy disappeared and a minute later returned with a bottle of Bayer.

I popped several pills and slid onto the couch. My back was my "cross to bear," as my mother had said all my life. The doctors couldn't say for sure, but they thought I was born with scoliosis, although it didn't present itself until I was around ten. *You look like a hunchback, Nancy. Stand up straight.* My father's words, carved in my brain, ever present. *You look like an old woman.* I willed myself to stay in the present, but my thoughts reinforced my desire to escape this town, my life, and most of all, my father. Small wonder I wasn't as happy as most of my friends. Except Peggy, but she hid behind her smile and blond Nordic looks. I guess I should be grateful that my dad never beat me or worse. Of course, spanking didn't count. Everyone got spanked.

"Still want to go shopping?" Peggy brushed invisible lint off the arm of the couch.

I'd forgotten we'd planned to walk downtown with Judy. "Mind if we skip it? Not in the mood, and it's too blasted cold. Since Dave will need Judy with him, I'll just head home." Shopping suddenly seemed meaningless in a world in which dead girls lie in snowbanks.

Maybe next week we'd hear what really happened at that party.

•   •   •

Half an hour later, I curled up in a ball in my basement sanctuary, the wind howling outside the window. My bedroom, a perfect escape from the clatter of everyday existence, was nothing fancy; concrete walls painted yellow, blue gingham curtains Mom sewed that I could pull aside on the small, rectangular window only displaying a pile of snow. Until I was twelve, I shared an upstairs room, begrudgingly, with my sister Robin, four years younger than me. I'd finally nagged my father into fixing up the empty room in the basement.

The only pleasing decor in my safe haven were prints of Van Gogh's *Sunflowers* and two Mary Cassatt's. I'd always loved them, especially Cassatt's portrayals of children and their mothers. I'd been lucky to find the prints at Ben Franklin's, a glorified junk store similar to Woolworth's minus the soda fountain.

Mom's eyes widened when I'd shown her the framed pictures. *They're so pretty, Nancy. You're a true Swede with all the blue and yellow.* At least she appreciated my efforts at a morsel of creativity.

One night at dinner, I'd tried to explain the Impressionists to my younger brother, Peter. My father scoffed and looked at Mom. *Hear that, Clara? Your kids go to college and think they know it all, too good for their parents, have their noses in the air.* I rolled my eyes, groaning. *Dad, we go to college to learn more and earn a good living.* I really wanted to tell him we attend college so we won't end up like him. But I bit my tongue.

. . .

I switched off the lamp, snuggled under Aunt Sigrid's quilt, and covered my ears. Trying to avoid images of Barbara, my thoughts drifted back to early childhood. Is that when it started? Walking through rooms, along sidewalks, into classrooms, pretty much unnoticed? As if apologizing for my presence in the world. When someone gives me a second glance, I think it's because of my curved back and my height. Do they think I slump on purpose to appear shorter? Judy would comment. *Stand up straight, Nancy. Be proud of your height. I wish I was taller.* Easy for her to say. Short and perky, she meant well, but her comments didn't help.

I never understood why she and Peggy included me as a friend. Judy, social and personable, and Peggy, blonde and sweet to everyone. And me? Drab brown hair, tall, humped over, too shy to talk in a group, especially with guys.

Of course, I was much luckier than some, like Lonnie Erickson from grade school. Poor kid had to stumble around in leg braces and one crutch due to polio. He had preferred reading in the classroom to watching the kids play during recess.

My life had to improve after I escaped this place. It had to, or else . . .

CHAPTER 4

Loreen
Saturday

The phone call this morning had thrown Loreen Sandberg into a tailspin. Her daughter, Judy, hung up gasping, "Oh, God, Dave just said the frozen girl they found dead was Barbara … Barbara Gruen."

"My God, you mean Dave's—"

"Of course, Mother, Dave's sister. Who else would it be?"

"Oh honey, I'm so sorry. Her poor parents and Dave too." Loreen wrapped her arms around Judy's shoulders. She couldn't fathom her future son-in-law's sister dying so suddenly.

"I know." Judy disentangled herself from her mother's embrace, wiping her eyes with her hands. "Dave's folks are on their way from Grand Rapids. They'll be here in an hour or so."

Loreen wondered where the Gruens would stay overnight. She'd be obligated to offer their guest room. But she hardly knew them. Reaching for a Kleenex on the kitchen counter, her eye twitched as she handed the tissue to Judy. "How could … nothing like this ever happens here. Why—"

"When is Dad coming home?" Judy sniffled.

"He's probably on the way from his coffee group." Loreen hoped so. Will was much better in a crisis. She reached for her pack of Salems, lit up, and inhaled deeply.

She and Judy sat on their ivory sofa, talking and waiting for Dave and Will to show up. Damn, what a situation. Loreen had been looking forward to a dinner party tonight at the home of a bridge club friend who'd invited two other couples as well. Eager to grace them with her presence, Loreen felt the opportunity slipping away. The couples belonged to the new country club and hopefully could recommend Loreen and Will for membership.

Why did this mess happen today? Now she'd have to cancel the dinner and wait for Lord knows how long to mingle with people of her pedigree.

•   •   •

Although Loreen had lived in Eklund for twenty-five years, she'd never adjusted to the place. The daughter of a successful architect, she grew up in Evanston, an affluent enclave of Chicago. When she met Will Sandberg, a handsome history professor at prestigious Northwestern University, she was smitten. Despite her parents' objections to her marrying a lowly professor, Loreen accepted Will's proposal after only six months of courtship.

Will's a nice fellow, but can he support you in the manner in which you've grown up? Her parents' words fell on deaf ears, and five months later, Loreen married Will in a small ceremony in her family's Episcopal church. Her mother lamented the modest wedding; she had dreamed of a Gatsby-like celebration for her attractive, red-haired daughter.

The birth of Will and Loreen's son in 1928 foreshadowed the family's relocating to northern Minnesota the following year after the stock market crashed. Will was furloughed from the university but soon found a teaching post at the teacher's college in Eklund. When Loreen balked at moving to a small town miles away from friends and family, Will tried to appease her. *Don't worry, dear. When things get better, we'll move back to Chicago. This is just a temporary situation.*

She recalled her father smoking his pipe in the living room right before they moved. *Will, tell me about this Eklund place. Sounds pretty isolated.*

Will straightened enthusiastically. *Yes, I suppose it is, but it's a unique town, right at the junction of railroads running north and south between Winnipeg and Minneapolis and east-west through Grand Forks and Duluth. All the grain and timber pass through Eklund.*

Loreen's mother had stifled a yawn and asked, *What do you know about the people there?*

Oh, they're just ordinary small-town citizens, but the town's surrounded by Indians, mostly Ojibwe, better known as Chippewa. White Earth, Thunder Lake, and Leech Lake Reservations form a triangle with Eklund at the center. The combined reservation populations outnumber the folks in Eklund two to one. The town still has a 'circle the wagons' feel to it.

Loreen cringed at Will's description; not likely to endear her parents to the place. He sounded like he'd rehearsed a lecture from his Minnesota history class. And, of course, he had to mention the Indians. What was the big deal about them?

After Judy was born in 1933, Loreen begged to return to Evanston. *Will, it's been three years. I have nothing in common with these people in this dinky backwater town. Can't we go back to Chicago and stay with Mother and Daddy until you find another job?*

• • •

Twenty-five years later, they still endured this frozen tundra, devoid of decent shopping, theaters, and art museums. However, Loreen still found Will's tall slim body, clear blue eyes, and Swedish bone structure able to charm her into staying.

At least Rod and Judy had turned out well, as far as she knew. Rod had graduated from the University of Minnesota and was happy in Minneapolis with his wife and baby. Judy, never a brilliant student, ended up at Eklund, majoring in elementary education. Her fiancé, Dave Gruen, football star, handsome, and amiable, would make a pittance teaching high school science. They planned to marry this summer, which left a few months for Judy to change her mind.

Meanwhile, Loreen longed for warmer weather. Chicago had never been this brutal. Even their cocker spaniel, Soldier, whined when forced to do his business outdoors in this Siberian hell.

Small towns, small minds, a cliché Loreen could concur with first hand.

CHAPTER 5

Nancy
Sunday

I awoke the next morning feeling more sluggish than usual, trying to process yesterday's news about Barbara Gruen. Too much for one day. Weird, fragmented dreams of snowmen, a California beach, and my father tearing apart a wigwam kept waking me. My blanket and sheets lay in a crumpled ball on one side of the bed.

Struggling from my cozy quilt, I thought of two essays I needed to complete today. But questions about Barbara preyed on my mind. I hoped to hear more details from Judy and Peggy today.

I slumped to the kitchen in my pink chenille bathrobe and wool stockings. The aroma of Mom's strong German coffee filled the air, and I poured myself a hefty cup.

"Bacon and eggs, Nancy?" She was already dressed for church, a well-worn apron covering her 1940s green wool suit.

"No thanks. I'll eat later." The thought of runny fried eggs gagged me. "Dad going to church?"

"Yes, he's supposed to usher today. Of course, he's griping about that."

Our family belonged to Our Savior Lutheran church, Missouri Synod, the one true church according to Mom and

Martin Luther. She remained proud of her German heritage, even after the war. Dad had reluctantly joined the church when they married twenty-six years ago and didn't seem to care which denomination. As long as it wasn't Catholic.

Through our grade school years, Peter, Robin, and I balked at mandatory church and Sunday school attendance every week. *Only the Catholic kids have to go every Sunday. Judy doesn't have to, and she's Methodist.* The arguments went on and on through the years. Finally, adolescence released us from the shackles of weekly church presence.

Mom would be shocked to know I never took her Lutheran religion seriously. Like how could a guy named Jonah spend three days in the belly of a whale and live to tell about it? Or perhaps it was four days. Hell if I knew.

I will say one thing for the Lutherans. We sipped wine for communion rather than watery grape juice the Methodists and Presbyterians imbibed, not to mention the Baptists.

The day dragged on at glacial speed. I finally finished both essays and planned to call Peggy, right when the phone jangled.

• • •

I lifted the receiver from the kitchen wall and tugged the long cord into the living room away from Mom's big ears.

It was Judy calling, her voice tight. "I still can't believe all this. Dave's folks came here yesterday, and … Nance, it was so awful. His mother was crying and his dad looked hollow. They're still in shock."

She took a breath. "They went to the morgue with Dave yesterday afternoon. He won't talk about that part. Before they got back, Mom started griping about what to do about dinner and resigning herself to letting them stay here overnight. Poor Mom." Judy's voice dripped sarcasm. "So put upon, so hard getting the guest room ready. With my help, by the way."

I said nothing, let her rant and rave.

Judy sniffled. "It's such a mess, we don't know what's going on. The Gruens and Dave just left for the police station to answer questions. Don't know what they're about."

"Does your dad know any more details? I think Barbara was in his class last quarter."

"His Civil War history class. Dave thought she might major in English. Oh God." Judy paused. "People at the college are talking about arranging a memorial convocation next week."

I twisted the phone cord into a knot. "Should Peg and I come over now? Keep you company till Dave and his folks get back?"

"Yeah. Thanks."

I figured Judy might prefer our company to her mother's. Loreen Sandberg was ... well, hard to explain.

•   •   •

The snow came down on huge cat feet as I clomped up Belby Avenue toward Judy's. In the late afternoon twilight, street lamps glimmered, and lights shone dimly through curtained windows along the way. Reminded me of a Currier and Ives winter scene. The words of a favorite poem floated through my mind. *The snow had begun in the gloaming, and busily all the night, Had been heaping field and highway with a silence deep and white.* Mom and I recited the first stanza of Lowell's poem each year when the first snowfall visited Eklund. Snow could be lovely for a poet lounging indoors by a fireplace, puffing on a pipe and admiring fir trees wrapped in ermine.

My thoughts sprang back to the present with children shrieking while playing "king of the hill" on a gigantic snowbank alongside the curb.

"I'm it, I'm it!" a boy in a roly-poly snowsuit hollered as his two playmates slipped and slid trying to dethrone him from his perch atop the mountain. I admired their apple-red cheeks and hoped their lives were as carefree as they seemed.

When I reached Judy's, she greeted me with a quick hug. Her vivacious cocker spaniel, Soldier, oblivious to my stooped posture, greeted me at the door as he yelped, jumped, and danced in circles. I bent down, petting the silky tan fur on his neck. "Always happy to see me, aren't you?" I loved the dog, and he loved me.

Judy and I joined Peggy, who sat in the color-coordinated living room decorated in ivory and peach. Or was it melon? A pleasant aroma from the fireplace, cigarettes, and gardenia-scented candles glided in the air.

Loreen and Dr. Sandberg talked over each other, beckoning me to come sit down, take off my coat, and other niceties. Loreen stood tall and elegant as usual, bottled red hair from the highest-priced beauty shop in town. A cigarette rested between her fingers, blood-red nails glossed to a sheen. "Come, girls, have some hot chocolate before you go chat. Oh, what a day this has been." In the kitchen she poured the simmering cocoa into our mugs. "Marshmallows?" she offered in a low, smoky voice.

We all declined and followed Judy up the stairs into her spacious bedroom, Soldier trailing behind. Her house far surpassed mine in size and furnishings, and Peggy's childhood home in the country was a shanty in comparison. Judy and I plopped on her double-sized bed, and Peggy pulled a green accent chair beside us and sat. The dog circled twice and lay on the rug, looking at us, one to the other, his long floppy ears framing endearing, soulful eyes.

"How are Dave's folks doing with all this?" Peggy asked.

"His mom finally quit crying and turned into a zombie." Judy leaned forward. "His dad acted almost normal, business-like, thanking us for the coffee Mom finally offered them."

After half an hour, I heard car doors slamming followed by voices downstairs. Hesitant to meet Dave's parents, yet aware of social protocol, I reluctantly followed Judy downstairs, Soldier trotting at my heels.

Everyone seemed to speak at once. Dave, usually handsome and robust, looked gaunt and gray. His father helped Mrs. Gruen shrug out of her brown wool coat. Dave introduced Peggy and me to his parents, while Will hurried to the kitchen to help Loreen get coffee ready.

Judy invited us to join everyone in the living room, but I thought we should leave. I mustered up the courage to speak to Mr. and Mrs. Gruen. "I'm so sorry about Barbara. She was a wonderful girl." I wished I could think of something profound to say to these good people who just yesterday had to identify their young daughter's body.

Mr. Gruen had the droopy jowls of a bloodhound. Had he always looked so sad? "Um, thanks for being here helping Dave. He'll really need his friends now."

Dave's mother gave us a vacuous stare, her red-rimmed eyes sank into her cheekbones. Short and bird-like, she managed a grimace and nod. Dave put his arm around her shoulder and guided her to the sofa.

"Sit down, Mom. They're bringing coffee and rolls. You should eat something."

"I don't ... I need to be ..." She could barely squeak out her words.

"I'll take her upstairs, son. She needs to rest for a while." Mr. Gruen took his wife's arm. "Come, dear. I think a nap would be good."

I marveled at his compassion toward her. I never witnessed that in my house.

"We'll leave now, Judy," I said. "Call us later."

As Peggy and I bundled into our parkas and boots, I heard a thump against the front door. I creaked it open, looked down, and whispered to Judy. "The *Post* is here. The paper boy just tossed it." I glanced at Dave and his father on the sofa.

"Let's see if there's anything in it." Judy stepped out, picking up the folded paper from the porch. "Shit, it's freezing out here."

The two of us huddled around her. There it was. Midway down the front page of the *Eklund Daily Post*. In bold letters: **College Girl found Frozen near Northlake Avenue**.

"What does it say?" I leaned in as we skimmed the article. "Damn, nothing we haven't heard already. It doesn't mention Barbara's name."

"Wait," Peggy said. "Look, at the end. It says that no foul play is suspected."

We looked at each other in puzzlement.

"Foul play?" I frowned. "Why would they say that?"

"I can't imagine," Judy replied.

CHAPTER 6

Nancy
Sunday

We said goodbye to Judy and walked down Callan Avenue until 15th Street, then went our separate ways. Late afternoon faded into twilight as uneasiness overshadowed me. What foul play could relate to Barbara? Why did the newspaper mention it, if she'd died from freezing?

When I came in the front door, Dad's trusty brown easy chair enveloped him. His long legs rested on the coffee table. He and Robin watched the CBS nightly news, my sister perched on the nondescript tan sofa. Pete was out somewhere, Mom in the kitchen. Where else would she be? I hung up my clothes and plopped on the sofa next to my sister.

"What did ol' Dr. Will Sandberg have to say about a student dying in his institution of higher learning, eh? The sacred halls of ivy aren't so sacred, are they?" My father had begun his requisite happy hour of Jim Beam and 7-Up.

I scoffed. "She died in a snowbank, not in the college, and Judy's dad didn't say anything new." I was not about to mention the 'foul play' comment from the newspaper. Dad wouldn't have read that, because he only subscribed to the Sunday *Minneapolis Star Tribune*. In his expert opinion, *the Eklund Post's a bunch of crap. Not worth the paper it's written on.*

On the news, Douglas Edwards somberly announced that Eisenhower was sending U.S. advisors to someplace called Vietnam.

"Damn TV. Fix it, will ya Robin?" Dad barked. The snowy black-and-white picture had rolled upward, typical of our lousy reception out here in the boonies.

"Stupid thing," whined Robin as she stood and stomped to the control dial on the TV. After fiddling back and forth with the instrument, the picture finally stabilized.

At eighteen, Robin was clearly my father's favorite. With her cornsilk hair and kitten blue eyes, she was a perfect picture of the classic Swedish maiden, as my granddad used to say.

All she needs are long braids, a blue gingham dress, and a milkmaid's yoke as she balances two pails of milk topped with thick cream. Granddad yearned for his homeland in Borlange.

Robin plopped back on the sofa. "Next time it's Nancy's turn to fix the dumb TV."

My father laughed. "Well, you're much better at it than Nancy. And she takes five minutes to get up from a chair." He took another swig of booze.

"Thanks, Dad." I'm sure my blood pressure rose. "I need a drink, that is if I can get up from the sofa."

"Aw, don't be so touchy. Your brother and sister can take a joke. Be more like them."

"Some joke," I muttered on my way to the kitchen for my version of a gin tonic. I poured nearly as much gin as 7-up in the glass. At least the ice trays were filled, so I wrenched several cubes into my hands, adding them to the cocktail.

Mom peeked over my shoulder. "That'll be pretty strong."

"Why don't you have one? You deserve it."

She puttered away, mixing ground beef and chopped onions for hotdish. "I'll probably have a glass of wine before dinner."

She reached for her pack of Kents and lit up. Somehow Mom could cook and smoke at the same time.

"Well, don't overdo it." I returned to the sofa, drink in hand, along with a plastic bowl of potato chips.

The news was wrapping up with Edwards's austere voice bidding everyone from coast to coast a good night from CBS.

"Guess it was too cold to go to the Muni last night, Nance?" Dad lit his pipe, the never-ending smell of Country Doctor tobacco, a permanent fixture in the living room.

"Yeah, Peg and I stayed in. In this weather, doubt if anyone would've been there." He'd referred to the Municipal Liquor Store on Third Street downtown where my friends and I often spent Friday or Saturday nights drinking a couple beers. After all, we were old enough. The store was dim, but inviting with a circular bar, booths and tables lining the sides, all in dark wood, attracting young and old alike.

Dad puffed his pipe, curls of grayish smoke circling over his head. "Yeah, only ones there would be the Indians. More of 'em are coming into town on the weekends to booze it up. Gotta watch out for them. After payday, they come off the reservation and drink up their wages."

"Daddy, that's not true," Robin piped up. "There are lots of good Indians. In fact, my friend, Lydia is—"

"I know. She's half Cherokee—"

"No, Chippewa. You're pretending not to know that. But they're really Ojibwe." Robin crunched potato chips indignantly, defending her friend. "But the common name is Chippewa."

Dad scoffed. "What's the difference, little Miss Professor? They're all the same. They should stay put where they belong. On Thunder Lake."

No use arguing with Dad when he voiced his whiskey-fueled opinions. Despite his ranting prejudices, Robin and I felt sorry for the occasional Indians we'd see shopping at Ben Franklin and the Red Owl grocery. Besides Roland, I'd never met any of them personally, but our junior high basketball teams would play against St. Catherine's Mission reservation school.

I never thought anything about Indians until several years later when I'd hear older people complain about the Chippewas' laziness and drunkenness. *Better watch out, Indian Joe might get you. Hey, there's Injun' Joe comin' outta the liquor store. Can't walk a straight line.* It wasn't until I turned thirteen, I realized Indian Joe wasn't a real person, but the representation of the whole tribe of Chippewa who lived at Thunder Lake.

Growing up, I guess we all thought of Indians as a group who lived apart, differently from us. We didn't view them as individual people. Sadly, they were like trees and roads in my peripheral vision.

But we were just kids. What did we know?

Judy called again after dinner. "Things are getting worse. Just got done telling Peggy." Judy choked.

I tightened my grip on the receiver. "Wha ... what happened?"

"The cops have been questioning the kids at the party again. Really drilling some of them. Including Barbara's friends." Judy seemed to choke again.

"How do you know that? Did you talk to her friends?"

"No, the cops stopped at our house right after dinner. Said they had more information, but told Dad they didn't want Barbara's parents to hear. The Gruens were upstairs for some much-needed solitude, so it was just Mom, Dad, Dave, and me in the living room."

I tried to get a handle on who was where. "So, the police told you about questioning Barbara's friends and the partygoers again?"

I heard Judy take a breath. "Yes, they said they were narrowing down, asking more specific questions. When we asked why, they said some new information had come to their attention."

"What information?"

Judy paused. "The medical examiner found something on Barbara's body."

CHAPTER 7

Loreen
Sunday

Loreen's sour mood worsened after the cops left, their intrusion delaying her dinner. They'd informed the family that strange markings were discovered on Barbara's body around the nose and face. Could be suspicious, but they didn't come out and divulge it. With more annoying investigations, Dave's parents would never go home. She guessed they'd be busy with funeral arrangements and paperwork during the days, but she'd need to prepare more meals and socialize with them. She couldn't fake sadness and sympathy, hated offering meaningless platitudes. But God knew she couldn't imagine losing Rod or Judy. Why couldn't she feel more compassion for these people?

Her thoughts drifted back to her ruined dinner plans last night. She knew her bridge friend understood why Loreen needed to cancel, but when would the opportunity arise again? The Eklund Town and Country Club had been completed two years ago, and Loreen had only finagled a few visits. She was still fishing for a member who'd sponsor her and Will for membership.

Her own faculty bridge club didn't help in that endeavor because those women hovered in the commonplace middle-class margins in Eklund's perceived hierarchy. Few if any of Will's colleagues belonged to the country club. Instead, the genteel members greeted business men, doctors, dentists, and, of course, old money like generations of furriers, railroad magnates, lumber tycoons, and the like. Academia, however, was a class unto itself. Loreen gritted her teeth through the monthly Wives Guilds, where she had little in common with women who shopped at JC Penney rather than O'Brien's.

Loreen echoed the same lament time and time again to her husband. *Will, there's no reason for us to be excluded from this rinky-dink town's country club. You've always liked to golf, and we have the money for dues.* She bit her tongue to keep herself from reminding him that her parents gave them generous monetary gifts whenever Loreen hinted at needing new furniture or a trip to Miami in wintertime. Maybe the membership committee figured college professors couldn't afford the fees. It couldn't possibly be her fault.

True, people already occupied their lives, but so few mattered.

CHAPTER 8

Roland

After bumping into Nancy on Saturday, Roland had waved goodbye as he bent his head against the ferocious, predatory wind. Since county road closures prevented driving to the reservation, his boss, Charlie, said he could work overtime on Saturday. Roland hoped he didn't run into the guys from the party last night. Barbara's death had not sunk in. He must hide his anxiety.

Thankfully, he had an easy day at the college. He'd sure lucked out when Hal Miles from the BIA and Judy's dad, Dr. Sandberg, arranged the job for him several years ago. The Bureau attempted to motivate Indian kids to make a better life for themselves. Miles had worked with Sandberg toward that goal. As a history professor, Sandberg had always taken an interest in America's Indian origins and the plight of their people.

Although Roland's job basically amounted to emptying wastepaper baskets and mopping floors, it beat bumming around with his buddies going nowhere. Besides, he could meet professors and students; Sandberg indicated the job could lead to Roland's auditing a few college classes in the near future.

After finally locking the maintenance cabinet with a satisfying click, Roland sighed in relief; he hadn't run into Albert

Melowski. His mind turned to the myth of Sally Roy's ghost, captured by Indians. It haunted the shores of Spirit Lake, warning children not to venture outdoors during a blizzard.

Roland stood shivering outside Main Hall for several minutes until Uncle Moose picked him up at 5 p.m.

"Get outta the cold," Moose croaked as Roland opened the passenger door of the battered brown '37 Chevy. Roland settled in the front seat, welcoming the heat. A blanket of snow masked the car's dents and scratches. As the car chugged out of the parking lot, his uncle squinted, avoiding several sky-high snowbanks.

A kind-looking man in his fifties, Moose's weathered face resembled the outer shell of a walnut, and his black eyes seemed on constant alert.

"Say, did you hear about the college girl who froze to death? Heard it on the radio. You know her?"

Roland shifted uneasily, straightening his back. "I don't think they've said who she was."

He disliked lying to his uncle, but he didn't want the older man involved. Too complicated. He shouldn't have to worry about his nephew. Moose had recently lent George, Roland's pa, money for a telephone, a luxury on the reservation. Moose was poor, but better off than George because he had no family to support. Roland didn't know the whole story, but he sensed the topic should remain unspoken.

Moose's old clunker continued to crawl along the snow-shrouded roads two miles toward the cabin.

"You know," Moose's voice gravely, "every so often you hear of folks freezing to death, especially if their car breaks down and they're in the boonies … nobody around for miles."

Roland studied the swirling flakes. "Yeah, I remember that guy off the reservation a few years back. Car got stuck in a snowbank, musta' been six feet high. Lost his way, skidded off the road."

"Yup, about ten years ago. Poor bastard. From the Cloud family." Moose coughed.

Suddenly, the car slipped on a patch of black ice. Like a seasoned pro, Moose casually steered it away from the ditch. He lifted his foot from the brake in order to keep the steering wheel straight as the car harmlessly glided over the ice.

They chugged onward. Roland thought of his friend, Jasper Pitts, who'd been along with him last night. Saw what he saw. They'd met up when Roland's shift ended and braved the snowstorm to walk downtown in search of an open bar. Fat chance of that. Then one thing led to another.

•   •   •

Back a few years during the summer, Roland had turned twenty-two and landed his college job. One sultry day, two skinny, pale-faced guys in torn jeans had stopped at Moose's bait shop where Roland helped out. The taller guy drove a decrepit tan junker, a '48 Ford F-1. The guys had slouched around the worn-down shelves, then asked to buy some leeches and minnows.

"Can we rent a boat?" the other kid asked.

"You know how to handle a row boat?" Roland didn't want to insult him, but asked anyway.

The taller one scoffed. "Those pieces of shit?" He waved toward two rickety wooden row boats tied to the dock outside. "Only problem, they'd fall apart in the middle of the lake."

The other kid nudged his partner, looked at Roland. "Sorry, my brother Donny here's an asshole sometimes. I'm Jasper, by the way." He turned to Donny. "Come on, them boats ain't gonna bust up in the lake."

The brothers returned to the shop several times that summer. Roland and Jasper talked about fishing, girls, money, or escaping to a big city like Minneapolis. Jasper had managed to graduate from high school, land a job at the Standard Oil station pumping gas, and gradually learned auto mechanics over the years. About the best a kid like him could do, living across the tracks, not setting the academic world on fire.

Sometimes Jasper borrowed his brother Donny's car, meeting up with Roland in the evenings after work. They'd go to the Muni for a beer or two, later bumming around town trying to stay out of trouble. Now and then they'd run into college guys or other working-class thugs who saw opportunity in the mismatched duo.

"Hey, skinny guy, you an' Injun Joe havin' a good time?"

Several of them knew Jasper from high school. "There's Jasper Pitts … you the pits … hey, your armpits stink."

When the jerks learned Roland's name, they'd continue their clever taunts. "Hey, nightbird brain. Scalped anybody lately? There's Roland Birdbrain. Whatcha doin' birdbrain?"

Roland was smart enough to ignore the insults; he told Jasper to keep his head down, cuss them out quietly, unheard. Gotta be unheard.

• • •

Roland jolted back to the present as Moose braked the car, creeping up his so-called driveway buried under snow. The wind pierced their bones as they huddled under parkas and hoods, making their way into the run-down cabin. Moose stoked up the woodstove, and the comforting aroma of smoky pine filled the air. They sprawled on the threadbare sofa, dotted with stains and cigarette holes. Moose had taped cardboard over the two ill-fitted windows and pulled together burlap curtains, attempting to keep the wind at bay.

"You an' Jasper go anywhere after the Muni last night?" Moose took a swig of Grain Belt.

Roland's heart jumped. "Nah, I told ya his car died, no phones to call you, so we hoofed it to meet you like we'd planned."

"Did ya go anywhere near the party house?"

"Don't think so. Why?"

"Ah, nothin' … jus' wonderin."

Roland wondered why his uncle was 'wonderin.' Fear clutched his throat. No way could Moose have seen anything. Not in that blizzard.

CHAPTER 9

Nancy
Sunday night

In the midst of Judy's phone call, I asked, "What? What could they have found on Barbara's body?"

"A … a crushed or broken nose, maybe something on her chin," Judy said. "The cop wouldn't come out and say it was foul play, but—"

"Oh, God, what caused it?"

"Jeez, Nance, I don't know. The medical examiner noticed her nose was crooked, leaned to the side, and on closer look, figured it was bent or crushed. The Gruens don't know about this, and Dad said I shouldn't tell anyone, so mum's the word."

That information was bound to leak out. I thought of Benjamin Franklin's aphorism: *Three can keep a secret if two of them are dead.*

"I won't tell a soul. Do you think Barbara was suffocated and didn't freeze accidentally?"

Judy sighed. "Sorry, I can't think anymore. Talk to you tomorrow. Bye." Judy hung up.

Did I detect irritation in her voice? Maybe I ask too many questions.

Monday

At eight-thirty in the morning, I lumbered my way through the ubiquitous snow to attend my classes. The wind had calmed, its anger abating overnight. A modicum of relief from the cold snap. Snowdrifts towered above my head as I plowed along a makeshift path on the sidewalk, stepping gingerly on footprints embedded in the snow by other shivering souls.

I nodded greetings to bundled-up students as I reached Pine Hall. After tugging the massive doorway open, I stamped grayish sludge from my boots onto the soggy rug inside.

Making my way through the sacred halls of academia to my classroom, I took extra care not to fall on the slippery floors and make a fool of myself. Clusters of students congregated in chattering, gossipy circles. I knew the entire campus would be buzzing about the latest news of Barbara Gruen.

I arrived at my Methods of Teaching English class, steeling myself for the tedium of another education course. Dr. Sulo Maki burst through the door several minutes late, looking more frazzled than usual in his attempt to straighten a pile of files in his arms.

He glanced at us, smoothing his Hemingway beard. "Hyvaa houmenta." He hailed his everyday greeting for six weeks now, a subtle reminder of pride in his Finnish heritage, the reasons unknown to me.

The professor plopped the files on his permanently cluttered desk. Adjusting his green wool tie around his neck, he continued. "I'm aware that it will be difficult to concentrate on the assignment this morning, given the tragic news we're all aware of. However, we will—"

A rapping at his chamber door interrupted his lofty insights. A pale-haired student aide wearing an orange knit sweater and plaid skirt entered, marched down the aisle, and handed Dr. Maki a sheet of mimeographed paper. She whispered something to him, then hurriedly exited the room.

Maki straightened his horn-rimmed glasses, glimpsing at the paper. "Well, students, this memo from the president's office is to be read in all classes, so that we shall do."

The students collectively perked up as he began. "First of all, we all send our heartfelt condolences to Barbara Gruen's family." He looked up at the class. "Perhaps some of you know Dave Gruen, Barbara's brother, who is a senior."

I looked down, rolling my eyes. Good Lord, everyone knew Dave; best point guard the school's had in years.

Maki cleared his throat. "Tomorrow morning at ten o'clock, there will be a memorial convocation for Barbara in Main Hall, with Reverend James Scribner of Calvary Lutheran Church officiating. The actual funeral service will be in Grand Rapids, Barbara's home town, this coming Friday, which will be for family and close friends."

He continued to inform us that the Administrators and Student committee is working on new guidelines regarding a buddy system for both on and off campus events. That is, students should not venture out alone during blizzard conditions.

I found it interesting the memo made no mention of having a so-called buddy to accompany anyone displaying symptoms of drunken behavior, trying to walk out alone in freezing temperatures. According to the brochures, the college provided a safe, upstanding environment to assure students a bright, successful future. President Harold Knox and his cohorts wouldn't tarnish the school's reputation nor risk lower enrollment, a possible result of the tragic accident. Perhaps other students shared my cynicism

• • •

After surviving my two morning classes, I headed for the admissions area to meet Peggy for lunch. We made our way to the student union cafeteria, where I grabbed a couple Cokes at the cash register. We found a table away from noisy students, and I opened my brown-bag lunch.

Unwrapping the crinkled tin foil from my ham and mustard sandwich, I noticed gray shadows under Peggy's eyes. "You tired, Peg?" Her face looked more pallid than usual.

She sighed. "Haven't been sleeping worth beans the last couple nights. Judy called early this morning with more information on what they found on Barbara." She brushed her wheat-colored hair behind her ear. "The cops didn't say it, but it sounds ... oh God, Nance, maybe she was strangled or smothered." Peggy took a deep breath, staring vacantly at her uneaten peanut butter sandwich.

"Yeah, when I talked to Judy, I thought the same thing." My cheeks turned hot. Nothing made sense anymore. "I still can't believe it. How could that happen in this little town? Especially to a girl like Barbara?"

Peggy sighed. "I don't know. Sounds like somebody ... Dave thought it could've been some drunk from the tracks or Indians. The cops are zeroing in on everyone who knew her. Not just kids at the party. Even teachers."

My stomach churned at the sight of my sandwich. I put it down, sipped my Coke. "I just don't know what to say anymore."

"I know." Peggy paused. "I lost my appetite. Don't even want my apple." She glanced around the room. "Judy also said tomorrow afternoon Loreen insists on going shopping for new black dresses for the funeral."

"Oh God, leave it to Loreen to worry about wearing the latest fashion to the poor girl's funeral."

"I have to work on Friday," Peggy sighed. "I could ask the boss for the day off, but I really don't want to make the trip to Grand Rapids. I don't own a black dress anyway."

"I'm sure Loreen would help you pick one out at O'Brien's, ha ha."

"Only if she'd foot the bill," Peggy scoffed.

I'd planned to attend the funeral. Judy and Dave were such good friends, and besides, it would honor Barbara. Also, a good excuse to miss my ed classes.

I thought more about Barbara. "I wonder about her body being taken out of town. I mean, will they have to keep it to examine it further? I saw on *Medic* where they did an autopsy on a guy who was stabbed, and they didn't release—"

"Oh, God, talk about something else. I can't stand thinking about that, so just let it go. I'm getting sick to my stomach."

Taken aback by her snappish tone, I put my sandwich in the bag and drained my bottle of pop. I'd been ready to mention that Sally Roy's ghost had returned to haunt the lake shores, but decided this wasn't the time for my dark humor.

"Sorry, Peg. I think the last couple days have made everyone edgy. Let's just go. We can't eat anyway."

Tears welled in Peggy's eyes as she shoved her untouched food in her paper sack. High cheekbones accentuated her sallow face. Had she lost weight? Something else troubling her?

We silently traipsed out of the union toward Peggy's office where I'd retrieve my parka before going to the library to study. I noticed Roland Nightbird sweeping the corridor, avoiding students tramping back and forth. He was going the opposite direction, so he didn't notice us. I tried to forget Dave's notion that perhaps an Indian had harmed Barbara.

I didn't know Roland that well, but I sensed he would never do such a thing.

CHAPTER 10

Loreen
Tuesday

Tuesday morning, Loreen stood in front of her closet, pondering what to wear for Barbara's memorial service at ten o'clock. Another obligatory task a good professor's wife must perform to keep up appearances. Since the service was in honor of Judy's fiancé's sister, she wouldn't dream of missing it. Well, maybe she would dream it, but in reality, not dare it. What would people think?

Her eyes traveled back and forth over her clothes as if she were watching a tennis match.

"I suppose everyone will wear black, but maybe a navy or gray dress would set me apart," she informed Soldier, who sat watching her, his amber-colored tail swishing back and forth. "Of course, later today, I'll buy a new black dress for the real funeral on Friday."

She peeled her eyes away from the closet and took in the luxurious atmosphere of her domain. Eight years ago, Loreen had insisted on re-decorating their master bedroom in blue with touches of pink and white. She tried to appease Will's complaints about the cost. She informed him they could well afford it, and his position as department chairman warranted a tad of luxury in their home.

Truth be told, Loreen only bloomed amidst lovely surroundings. She needed … no, deserved an elegant room. After all, she was still stuck in this backwater town because she was a good, supportive wife to Will.

Yes, she was a queen in her chamber of blue and white papered walls. White floor boards and matching crown molding accented navy wall-to-wall wool broadloom carpeting. A silky ice blue bedspread lay in splendor atop the bed, showcased with a ruffled sapphire bed skirt and matching tufted headboard.

A tap on the half-closed door interrupted Loreen's reverie. "Mom, you'll be late. Better hurry."

Loreen checked her gold watch. "Plenty of time. As you know, the wives will proceed up the hall with their husbands and sit in the front." She bent down to rub Soldier behind his floppy ears. "We need to provide a united front and all that." She didn't mention what a farce the silly tradition was.

Judy plopped down on her mother's favorite piece of furniture. A tufted white silk chez longue rested against an imposing bay window. The eastern sun streamed in, which highlighted the grandeur of the Victorian-style chair, the piece de resistance of Loreen's self-perceived elitism. Not to mention her correct usage of French pronunciation.

Loreen eyed Judy. "Careful, honey. Keep your shoes off."

Judy rolled her eyes. "My one shoe is five inches away. Don't worry, it still looks like Cleopatra is sitting here."

"Yes, I remember that's what Nancy said when she first saw this. That it's fit for Cleopatra." Loreen beamed.

"I know, I know," Judy said. "I'll leave in a minute and ride to the memorial with Dave and his dad. Mrs. Gruen can't face going, so she's staying at the motel."

Loreen had felt a twinge of guilt when the Gruens had checked into the White Birch Motel on Northlake, several blocks away. But she'd eased her conscience by convincing herself of an unspoken understanding that separate accommodations would allow more privacy, and Barbara's mother obviously needed to be alone in her grief.

Loreen scrutinized her daughter. "Is that what you're wearing?"

Judy glanced down at her dark green sweater and gray pleated wool skirt. "What's wrong with this? For your information, Mom, college kids don't dress up like old ladies."

"Don't be fresh." Loreen continued to study her own wardrobe. Judy had a mind of her own and showed little interest in the finer things in life. As a mother, where had she gone wrong?

•　•　•

After the convocation, Loreen had to allow it was nicely done. Reverend Scribner's message was thankfully short, and college President Harold Knox and the student dean refrained from droning on ad nauseam, no doubt currying favor with the audience.

The college choir performed "In the Garden" and "How Great Thou Art," which Loreen found meaningful in spite of herself.

Afterward, everyone trailed out of the assembly, stopping to greet friends and acquaintances.

"Mom, Dad," Judy called as they entered the lobby. She waved, and as they met, gave Will a hug, then Loreen.

"Hi, Sweetheart," Will said. "Lovely service, wasn't it?"

Judy sniffled, her eyes rimmed in red. "Yes, it was." She eyed her mother's outfit, a gray wool suit with a foxtail neck wrap. The poor fox looked none too happy, its tiny teeth baring a grim smile. "You certainly did outshine the other women, Mom."

Loreen scoffed, secretly pleased, and handed Judy a tissue. "I'm sorry, honey, it must've been so hard for the family and you too."

Judy wiped her nose. "I really got choked up when we sang "Abide With Me" at the end.

The hymn had touched Loreen, but not to the point of tears.

Will added, "A Mighty Fortress is Our God" always gives me a lump in my throat too."

Judy dabbed her eyes again. "Mom, I better get back to Dave and Mr. Gruen. Not sure what we're doing next, but you and Dad can go on home. I'll call you later."

Loreen smiled and nodded, relieved the event was over, and she could be alone. She hoped they'd all have lunch downtown.

•　•　•

At one o'clock, Loreen and Judy sat at the kitchen table discussing afternoon plans.

Judy gently blew on her coffee, then sipped. "Last night I invited Nancy to go shopping with us today for a black dress. Actually, she only needs a black skirt or sweater."

"Oh, really," said Loreen, disappointed. "Can she afford O'Brien's?"

"Don't be so snooty. Nancy isn't poor, you know." Judy took a molasses cookie from a china plate and bit into it.

"I know, but …" Loreen stopped herself. She and Judy had known the salesladies in O'Brien's for years. What would they think seeing Nancy with them? Not that the poor girl was that shabby, of course.

Judy continued. "So, I told Nance we'd meet her at the store around two-thirty, all right?" Loreen's swallowed hard and nodded her compliance.

Lord, would this week ever be over?

CHAPTER 11

Nancy
Tuesday

Everyone I spoke to agreed that Barbara's memorial service was very well-done without sentimental gushing from the speakers. The resounding chords of the organ, the hymns, and especially the choir, all impressive. Standing in the lobby after the service, I spotted Peggy mingling and waved at her. She either didn't see me, or ignored me. We hadn't spoken since yesterday when she snapped at me over my comments about transporting Barbara's body. Oh well.

I ran into Judy, Dave, and Mr. Gruen in the lobby where we exchanged kind words about the service. I felt profound sympathy for all of them, especially Barbara's dad. His sagging eyes bore pools of tears.

Judy's lips curved downward, twitching. She took a deep breath, taking me aside. "At least our shopping trip this afternoon will take our minds off things for a little while."

"That's true," I said. "We're still meeting at O'Brien's about two-thirty?"

"Right." Judy touched my arm and turned to greet others.

I had Applied Psychology class before lunch, so I bounded toward another stimulating lecture. Yes, my ridicule got the best of me at times.

Walking home afterwards, I noticed the wind had died down and the temperature graduated from freezing-ass cold to just freezing cold. When I opened my front door, a whiff of chicken soup greeted me.

In the kitchen, my father was finishing lunch and pushed back his chair. "How was the funeral?"

I groaned. "It wasn't a funeral, Dad. A memorial convocation. Barbara's funeral will be in Grand Rapids on Friday."

"Well pardon me, miss high and mighty." He belched, softly for once. "Now, if you'll excuse me, I have just enough time for a pipe before going back to the salt mines." Dad was station master at the Great Northern Railroad downtown. He wore his typical long-sleeved shirt and gold pocket watch, its chain looped downward, clipped to his black vest.

Mom scurried around the kitchen. "Sit down, Nancy, and warm up. Tell me about the memorial; who spoke, the music, everything." She put a bowl of steaming chicken and vegetable soup on the table, sat down, and lit up a Kent.

I told her about the service, and also my plans to meet Judy and Loreen at O'Brien's to shop for black dresses for the funeral. Mom paused. "Why do you need a black dress?"

"I don't, but I could use a black skirt or a new black sweater."

Mom raised her eyebrows. "I've rarely set foot in O'Brien's. I don't feel comfortable."

I shook my head. "You're too worried about the cost, but they have good sales sometimes."

She shrugged. "The clerks think they're so highfalutin, it's like they owned the place."

"From the looks of your clothes, Nance, you can use all the help you can get," Dad blurted from the living room.

"Just how long is his nose?" I whispered to Mom. "Try to have a private conversation around here." Lord, I couldn't wait till June when I'd finally fly this coop.

"Theo, leave her alone. I'm glad she has more confidence than me. Besides, there's nothing wrong with her clothes."

I could always count on Mom to come to my defense. "See you later." I patted her hand. "I'll clear the table and do some homework."

. . .

I arrived at O'Brien's early, opened the door, and wandered in. The shop was one floor with a basement for children's clothing. Stark white walls exuded a clean, bright atmosphere.

I moseyed around a small table of stockings, gloves, and similar outerwear. I held up a pair of black leggings, feeling their soft, wooly texture.

"May I help you?" A middle-aged woman peering through tortoise-colored glasses had sidled beside me.

I jerked my head up. Where had she come from?

"No thank you, I'm just waiting for—"

"The clearance rack is over there." She gestured to an area along the opposite wall. "Some items are up to sixty percent off."

I stood eye-to-eye with the phony old bag. I knew her type, appraising me the moment I'd walked in. I willed myself not to tell her off. Instead, I said, "Like I tried to say, I'm waiting for a couple others."

Her tight, forced smile did not reach her beady squirrel eyes as she huffed off to pounce on another unfashionable soul.

"Nancy." Judy's voice came as a breath of fresh air.

"Hello, dear." Loreen touched my arm, casing the shop like Dick Tracy.

I greeted them and pointed toward the opposite wall. "The clearance rack," I started in the snobbiest voice I could manage, "is over there. Sixty percent sale."

Judy giggled. Loreen looked confused.

We proceeded toward the back of the store where Dior, Chanel, and Givenchy awaited Eklund's posh women.

"Hello, Loreen," a tall woman with bleached blond hair and sculptured Aryan cheekbones gushed. "How have you been?"

"Oh, you know ..." her words fading away.

"You've had a difficult time. I'm so sorry about your, a—"

Loreen sighed. "Yes, Dave's sister, Barbara. A real tragedy." She looked at Nancy. "Nelda, this is Judy's friend, Nancy Borg."

I gave a half smile and an awkward nod.

"Hello, Nancy. I think I've seen you in here before. Hard to keep track of the young ones." Nelda's careful face looked as if it had been rinsed with vinegar. "What can I do for you ladies today?"

Loreen told her she and Judy were looking for black dresses for Friday's funeral, and Nancy was, well, looking for something black.

At one point when Loreen and Nelda fluttered around the dressing area, I quietly asked Judy, "Have you heard anything more about the investigation?"

Judy pursed her lips. "Not really. The cops are still questioning Barbara's friends more closely, especially those at the party. Also, her professors for some reason. Guess they may have overheard something."

"Overheard what?" I sensed Judy's impatience with my questions. "I don't know. I can't think about it right now. We need to get through the week and let the dust settle."

I knew I should drop the subject and had no choice when Loreen appeared. Strands of her Lucille Ball hair escaped from her sculpted bun, circling down her neck. "Judy, I found a couple dresses for you to try on. Nelda thinks they'll be perfect for you."

Judy leaned toward me, whispering, "Nelda Whitney thinks she's the next Coco Chanel."

"Yeah, I know her kind."

Twenty minutes later, we left the hallowed portals of O'Brien's and headed to our cars. Loreen and Judy had found basic black cashmere dresses, and, much to the satisfaction of the clerk who'd greeted me, I'd ended up at the dreaded clearance rack choosing a charcoal gray pencil skirt with kick pleat. And it was even fifty percent off. All without Nelda's approval, who wouldn't be caught dead rifling through sale items in any store.

• • •

That evening I thought about tomorrow and what awaited us. I had volunteered to help the Gruens and Judy clear out Barbara's dorm room.

Glad to help in any way I could, I still dreaded the prospect. However, I admired the family's strength and dignity despite their lives being shattered three short days ago.

CHAPTER 12

Roland
Tuesday

After the memorial service, Roland had helped two other workers lug the podium off the stage of the assembly room. They folded up and cleared off a dozen or more chairs, pushing them away on two large platform carts for storage. They returned to sweep the floors and tidy the place after everyone left.

Roland knew the day would be painful. A final tribute to a special person. To Barbara. During the ceremony, he'd dilly-dallied in the east section of the building, trying to appear busy. On his way back for clean-up, the stirring melody of "Beautiful Savior" caused him to stifle the urge to turn around and go anywhere but there. He couldn't wait to meet his pal Jasper after work.

• • •

Later, as Roland climbed into Jasper's old Ford beater, his friend asked, "Any more news today about—"

"Naw, didn't hear more rumors." Roland reached toward the dashboard and turned up the heat.

They drove down Timber Drive toward town. At least the roads were plowed with no new snow. It even felt warmer; maybe spring was in the air? Fat chance of that.

Jasper sputtered along until they reached his weather-beaten house by the railroad. Lund Street, one of the poorest in town, ran parallel to the tracks heading east toward Cass Lake and beyond.

He and his brother, Donny, still lived at home with their mother to save money for their own place someday. She worked as a maid during the days and drank during the evenings. Never got hangovers, lucky for her.

Jasper led the way up a narrow, snow-packed sidewalk and tugged open the rickety wooden door. The roof hid under a carpet of white, and the yellow wood siding probably hadn't been painted since the Hoover administration.

"Ma," Jasper called as he pulled his gray knit hat off his straw hair. "We're ready for supper."

Roland shut the door, pulling it a couple times to make sure it closed tightly. A scent of beef stew and cigarettes drifted in the air.

"Hold your horses." A stout, middle-aged woman with wispy gray hair emerged from the kitchen into the postage stamp of a living room. "Oh, hi, Roland. You two behaving yourselves?"

"Hello, Elsie." Roland shook off his parka, smiling at the woman. Usually grumpy, surprisingly she'd always been cordial to him. He wondered why she never seemed to object to Jasper's friendship with an Indian.

"Come on, warm up, have some Sunday stew, even though it's Tuesday. Been cookin' for hours. Old lady Thomas sent me home this morning cuz she's sick. Sick in the head if you ask me. Anyway, I got almost a whole day off." A cigarette dangled from the corner of her pencil-thin lips. "Wanna beer?"

"Yeah, thanks." Roland liked and respected Elsie, who had supported the family since the war when Jasper's father lost his life in 1944 at Omaha Beach.

"Got any Hamm's?" Jasper asked.

"Wasn't talking to you," Elsie cackled.

"Ah, Ma." Jasper grinned at Roland. "Always kidding around."

Elsie turned toward the kitchen. "Is Grain Belt good enough for your highness? On sale."

"Sounds good," Roland said. "Need any help with supper?"

Elsie snorted. "Why don't my no-account sons have manners like that?"

"Ma, you know we work around here. Roland's gonna think we're lazy bums."

Elsie set two Grain Belts on the table and picked up her own half-empty bottle. She took a swig and put it back by her chair. "I'll get your grub from the kitchen."

She placed three chipped bowls and stainless spoons on the oilcloth table cover decorated with roosters, hens, and chickens in every color imaginable.

Roland tossed down a swig of beer. "That sure smells good, Elsie."

She carried a cast-iron pot of stew and placed it on a large crocheted hot pad, blistered with browned stains. "Here ya go, boys. Dig in."

She insisted Roland help himself first, and soon they were all slurping beef stew, swimming with carrots, sliced potatoes, onions, and other chunks of food Roland couldn't identify. He savored the spicy flavors, perfect for a chilly night.

"Got any bread, Ma?" Jasper's mouth was full.

"Gott in Himmel, I'm not your slave. Get it yourself." Gravy dribbled onto her red gingham housedress.

Jasper returned holding three slices of white bread in one hand, a plate of butter in the other. Then back for knives.

"You forgot the napkins," Elsie chided.

Jasper groaned, retrieved three paper towels he folded in half at the table. "Satisfied now, Ma? Can I sit my as—butt down and eat in peace?"

"Yeah, set your ass down, son. Ya done good."

• • •

Later, Jasper led the way to the basement where he and Donny shared an unfinished square bedroom. Concrete walls and a mud floor surrounded twin beds covered with rumpled gray blankets. Four orange crates hugging the walls served as dresser drawers. A green and orange afghan, wool threads trailing around its edges, rested askew at the bottom of Donny's bed. He was out of town, so Roland would use his bed for the night.

Roland attempted to straighten the afghan and flopped onto the mattress. Jasper lay on his side atop his own tangled covers. They'd grabbed another beer just for good measure.

"You sure you didn't get wind of anything more on the investigation?" Jasper took a swig.

"No," said Roland, impatient. "But the thing is …" He lowered his voice. "We need to get our stories straight. I'm sure nobody saw us, but you never know. They'd tell the cops for sure."

Jasper stretched out his lanky body, long feet dropping over the end of the bed. "Naw, I don't see how anyone else was out there in the blizzard. Couldn't see shit."

"Well, Einstein, we saw ahead of us. I told ya before, I'm sure it was Albert Melowski. Got a glimpse when his hood blew off for a second, but don't blab. Then we'd be in hot water for being there."

"I won't, but I'd sure like to see that big college football star get his ass knocked down a peg."

"Yeah, but listen to me. I made up an alibi for us just in case."

"So what's our story gonna be?" Jasper guzzled his beer. Roland absently folded and unfolded the wooly afghan while he concentrated on their plan. He took a gulp from his bottle.

"I've thought about this for a few days, and here's the deal. First, never tell anyone the truth. Not Donny, no one. Now, here's our story."

CHAPTER 13

Nancy
Wednesday

I woke up groggy as ever and sat up in bed to get my bearings. I thought of late yesterday when Mom had admired my new gray wool skirt after I returned from my big shopping spree at O'Brien's. Robin had to appraise the skirt as well.

"Wish I could afford that store," my sister had exclaimed.

"Don't be too impressed … it was on sale."

Mom fondled the smooth fleecy fabric. "We shouldn't act like we're not good enough for them. Their customers are no better than we are."

"No, just richer," I said. Robin and I snickered.

I'd had enough for the day and didn't want to sit at the dinner table with my father around, so I'd told Mom we'd stopped for sandwiches at Rex Café. I wasn't hungry, which I used as an excuse to bolt downstairs to my basement haven for the night.

• • •

Today, I had volunteered to help clear out Barbara's dorm room. My Methods class ended at 1:00, so I'd meet Judy, Dave, and his dad, Ed, at the room in Tamarack Hall. The building stood on the north side of the grade school across Birchfront Drive, a walk of only a couple blocks.

On my way to the dorm, I wondered what occupied Martha Gruen during the days when her husband and son were tending to Barbara's final arrangements. I doubted Loreen would lend a helping hand of comfort and support, or hell, even a cup of coffee.

The sidewalks had turned slick with glassy frosting. Even though they'd been sanded, I still needed to step gingerly. My damn back occasionally affected my balance, especially in the cold. At least it wasn't so frigid today, and even the sun tried to climb above towers of Norway pines shadowing Spirit Lake. When did I last see the sun? Damned if I knew.

I arrived at the two-story red brick building and arduously climbed the stairs to the second floor. Several girls in wool skirts and heavy pullover sweaters ambled down the hall, one or two trying not to stare at the folks milling around Barbara's room. Other people's adversity always attracted the curious like a magnet. Human nature, I guess.

"Hi, Nancy." Will Sandberg stood like a sentry at the door, his tie loosened over his white shirt and corduroy jacket. He never seemed to age; he looked the same as when I was a kid, handsome, few if any wrinkles, an air of Cary Grant about him.

"Hello, Dr. Will." I shrugged out of my parka and peered through the door. "Are they ready for me?"

Judy appeared and said, "Come in, Nancy. Don't just stand there. Got work to do."

I liked the idea of working as a team, doing something tangible rather than sitting around talking about the tragedy. I stepped in, tossed my parka and book bag on a folding chair, and rolled up my sweater sleeves to my elbows. The room smelled of Pond's talcum power and unbearable grief.

I greeted Mr. Gruen, who stood forlornly at the closet door, seeming to study the air around him. Dave bent over a cardboard box, opening the top.

"Nance," he said, "thanks for coming. Barbara's roommate's staying in a spare room down the hall till things get ... ah, settled."

I hadn't thought about the roommate and didn't want to start now.

"I've already begun one box of bath things." Judy indicated a smaller box with cosmetics, shampoo, toothpaste and such. "I thought you and I could pack up her other personal things, like clothes. Put some in her suitcases, some in boxes. Plus, the linens."

"Good plan." I was determined to concentrate on the job itself and not Barbara's knickknacks and broken dreams. Gotta distance myself.

Dave stood. "Here's another box to use. Dr. Will, Dad, and I will cart the boxes and other stuff and load up the car." He leaned toward me and shook his head as he gestured to Ed.

The poor guy looked as though he'd been struck in the head, a pitiful shell of a man. I hated to imagine the state of his wife.

"I'll take this out, Dad," Dave said as he lifted a small white veneer table. "God, she had this thing since she was a kid." His blue eyes moistened, and sweat glued his brown hair to his forehead.

Judy reached in the closet and carried several skirts to the bed. She removed the hangars. "I'll keep at the clothes, Nance, and you can start with the top dresser drawer. Most of that can go in the suitcases, and I'll put the clothes in boxes."

"All right," I murmured. A suitcase lay opened on the floor, and I pulled out a dresser drawer. I gingerly smoothed small mounds of pink and white underpants along with other lingerie. I felt as if I were invading Barbara's privacy and something more than that. Then it came to me: her dignity. I slowly lifted two bras with pointy cups, an open-bottom girdle, and two slips, placing them in the suitcase. The nylon fabric of the slips and pants felt soft and satiny, even the stretchy mesh girdle.

Ten minutes later, I'd emptied the dresser of flannel pajamas, knit socks, and a pair of long johns that her mother had coerced her into bringing. "She never wore them," Judy said. "But Dad wears them on the weekends."

I refused to wear them. "They're for men," I'd said to Mom, trying to justify my viewpoint.

I stuffed the suitcase with long-sleeved shirts and sweaters, while Judy continued filling boxes with skirts, jackets, and slacks.

I said, "I'll take the sheets off. Will Martha want to keep them?" I wondered what use they'd be.

"Yeah, we'll take them. They can donate 'em later to the church if they want."

I shrugged the pillowcase off, then untucked the white cotton sheets. I reached under the mattress to tug the bottom ends out and felt something hard. My fingers encircled the corner of a leathery small object. A booklet? My hand slid further under the mattress and felt the edges of a book with a metal clasp on the side. I grasped a corner of it and pulled.

In my hand rested a small maroon vinyl journal with a gold latch and tiny key hole. It must have been a diary, like young girls have, except no words or decoration appeared on the cover. Surprised, I turned toward Judy, her head down, folding corduroy slacks. I nearly revealed my discovery, but something unexplained held me back. Why did I want to keep silent? Maybe I wanted to preserve Barbara's privacy, to honor her final thoughts on this earth. Or protect her from others, even family, reading it?

I tucked the book in my purse. I'd probably give it to Judy later.

Uneasiness and guilt crept into my mind as I finished folding the sheets. I kept an eye on Judy, still busy filling her box.

"Is there room for the sheets?" My voice must have indicated my sudden breathlessness.

Judy turned and stared at me. "You okay, Nance? You look pale."

"Yeah. Guess I wasn't prepared for the ... the emotion." I choked on the words. Oh God, I didn't want to cry, but my lips quivered and my throat tightened. I sat slumped on the bed with my face in my hands and gave up, allowing my tears to flow.

"Oh, Nancy," said Judy as she sat beside me, circling an arm around my shoulder.

"I'm sorry," I sniffled. "I didn't see this coming." I felt like a weakling. We couldn't cry in my house without Dad calling us bawl babies.

"It's all right. I've shed many tears the past week." Judy handed me a Kleenex. "We're all tired and shocked and can't see straight. It's normal to feel weepy."

I blew my nose. It was unusual for me to lose control like that. Oh well, I'd get over it. At least the men were busy and didn't notice. Except poor Ed Gruen may have.

•   •   •

Within an hour, Dr. Will, Judy, and Dave were finishing up and hustled me out of the room. I'm sure they wanted some privacy, and Judy knew I was on my last leg.

And so, I dragged myself toward home, the day's early dusk hung gray and depressing. My boots crunched on the glazed sidewalk. The snow lay sleeping away, no longer hurling from the sky. The smell of woodsmoke filtered through the air.

I clutched my purse, harboring the secret inside. I'd hide the diary in my bedroom. Find a spot no one would discover. But could I resist the temptation to read it?

CHAPTER 14

Loreen
Wednesday

The morning dawned a somber gray. Groaning, Loreen sat up in bed, planted her feet on the floor, and braced herself for another day of aggravation. She heard water running in the bathroom; Will would be out in a minute, bright-eyed and bushy tailed, as her mother would say.

Sure enough, Will, annoyingly cheerful, came in the bedroom. "Good morning, dear. You go back to bed. I'll get my own breakfast."

"I am pretty groggy," Loreen answered. "I may do just that."

Will chose a shirt and tie from the closet. "You had a restless night … even talked in your sleep."

"Oh Lord, what did I say?"

"I'll never tell." He chuckled as he bent down and gave her a peck on the cheek.

Loreen feigned a slap on his back side. "Oh, you beastly man. Just for that, I'll sleep until noon."

No matter how much she detested Eklund and its wretched winters, Will was the reason she continued to tolerate the place. She knew in her heart she didn't deserve him.

• • •

Mid-morning the doorbell rang, and Loreen's old (in more ways than one) friend, Alma breezed in, the aroma of her signature Yardley Lavender whispering in the air. Alma had called earlier saying she'd just baked her special peanut butter cookies and was bringing some over to share.

Loreen happily poured coffee at the kitchen table and placed the still-warm cookies on a china plate.

"Yum, delicious," Loreen cooed, as she bit into a thick gooey cookie. "I'll have to get the recipe."

"Yes, they're quite easy." Alma, the widow of former college president, Harry Schneider, had been kind and welcoming to Loreen from the beginning. Alma still lived in their spacious, Art Deco home on the lake after Harry's heart attack ten years ago.

Loreen sipped her coffee. "I'm glad you came over, Alma. What a week I've had." She shouldn't complain, though, since Alma was no stranger to death and grief.

"I know, you poor dear," she purred in her silver-spoon voice which complemented her aristocratic cheekbones, creamy complexion, and arctic white hair sculpted into a bun. She wore a pearl-colored cashmere sweater and tailored wool slacks.

After reaching for her pack of Salems, Loreen held it toward Alma, who accepted a cigarette, her hand marbled with purple veins.

Loreen lit their cigs with her crystal lighter, and both women puffed away.

"What's the latest news on the investigation?" Alma asked.

Loreen paused, flicking an ash into a chartreuse glass ashtray. "Well, I know you'll keep this confidential, but yes, some names have come up." She'd mentioned the possible fracture on Barbara's nose to Alma yesterday.

Alma lifted her penciled eyebrows. "Do tell, and of course, I won't breathe a word." She peered at Loreen through round hazel eyes.

"Well, the police said that they zeroed in on a boy from the party and maybe a witness who saw him afterwards."

"Oh, Lord, you mean after the party ended? In the blizzard?" Alma inhaled and blew rings of smoke in the air.

"I guess so. It seems the guy left after Barbara did. At first no one acknowledged seeing her leave by herself, but someone told someone else and the police … oh God, Alma, I'm so rattled and confused I don't know who said what." Loreen crushed her cigarette in the ashtray, hand trembling. "More coffee?"

"Please," said Alma. "Does Will know the boy? Did the police say who he was?"

"Oh, let's see … a kid named Albert something." Loreen fetched the percolator and poured them another cup. "The kid was a student of Will's a year or two ago. So, I guess he's not an Indian."

Alma's eyes widened. "Oh, do they think an Indian had something to do with it?"

"Not really. I must've heard a little something though." Loreen lit another Salem, drew in deeply, and lifted her face to exhale ribbons of smoke toward the ceiling.

"Well, I wouldn't put it past him. Except, what would an Indian be doing at a college party?" Alma smoothed back an imaginary wisp of hair.

"I guess he could've been walking home from the Muni. Lord knows, they drink up their welfare money on Friday nights." Loreen knew that wasn't accurate for all of them, but close enough.

Alma shifted in her chair. "They are a sorry lot, for sure. Always been a bane on society."

Loreen sighed, shook her head. "I've hardly ever run into any, but Will has helped one or two over the years. He knows a man from the BIA and they … you don't want to hear the whole boring story."

"Maybe not," Alma said. "Oh, then there's that silly myth that's been around for years about the Indians and the ghost of that little girl Sally Roy they found frozen. Maybe there was a connection of sorts."

"Lord, you believe in ghosts?" Loreen teased.

"Oh, don't be daft. I meant maybe the myth started because someone saw something suspicious."

Loreen gave a half chuckle. "You've been watching too much *Alfred Hitchcock Presents*."

"Could be, my dear." Alma stood. "Keep in touch. I must run off. My hairdresser awaits."

She was off in a flurry of waves and Yardley Lavender.

•   •   •

Afterward, thoughts of Indians niggled in Loreen's mind. She'd learned from Will that the Chippewas at Red Lake were actually Ojibwe, along with an unpronounceable mile-long word starting with an *A*, probably used by scholars. Although she didn't share her husband's empathy toward Indians, she had never met one, nor given them a second thought until now.

At least they were nothing like the blacks who infiltrated their way into Chicago, mostly the south side. No problem for her parents in Evanston. Oh, how she missed that place. Would she ever think of Eklund as home? Highly doubtful, especially after this recent upheaval in her life.

And all because her future son-in-law's sister Barbara died and made a fine mess of things.

CHAPTER 15

Roland
Wednesday

Roland jolted awake, momentarily forgetting he'd slept in Jasper's brother's bed. Elsie crowed down the basement stairs, "Jasper, get up. You'll be late for work. Got oatmeal ready."

"Shit." Jasper groaned, uncovered his eyes. "You awake, Roland?"

"Barely," Roland grunted. "Drunk too much beer last night. What time is it?"

"Almost seven. Gotta hurry if I'm gonna drop you off at the college before work." Jasper kicked off his covers. "I'll head upstairs and wash up. Won't take long."

Last night they'd spread out on the blankets, drinking and talking. He'd coached Jasper on their alibi, but Roland wasn't convinced his friend would remember the details. Because the cops had been asking more questions, Roland's gut told him they should hurry up with a solid story. Didn't hurt to be on the safe side.

• • •

After wolfing down their oatmeal and coffee, they threw on their parkas.

"Come back soon, Roland," Elsie chirped. "Good for Jasper to have a friend."

"I will, thank you." Why he couldn't have a mother like that?

Outside, another gray-ceiling winter day awaited them, a white shroud covering the outdoors, silent and secret.

Roland shivered, not so much from the cold, but from something inside him. Something sinister. He thought of his uncle Moose who claimed his great grandfather had been a Mide, or medicine man. Roland had heard childhood stories, especially during wintertime, how the Mide not only healed the sick or injured, but sensed when trouble would descend on the tribe. He'd warn the village folks of impending danger, either man-made or natural. He'd alert tribal leaders of imminent attacks from the Sioux or Lakota, as well as approaching blizzards, freezing rain, severe thunderstorms, hail, and floods.

Roland figured Moose had consumed too much firewater while reminiscing about the good old days.

"What's the story again?" Jasper interrupted Roland's thoughts as they chugged along toward the college. "Damn heater ain't workin' yet."

Roland's saw his breath fogging the air when he opened his mouth to talk. "Gotta listen hard, and don't forget. Here's what happened." He repeated his story, slowly and deliberately to Jasper as they skirted patches of ice and slowly approached stop signs.

They would tell the cops that they'd been to the Muni on Friday night and left when it closed early at 10:00. They'd claim they were pretty plastered, that Jasper slowly drove them to the college where Moose would meet Roland and drive him to Moose's place. They'd omit the part about Jasper's car on the fritz. The storm hadn't hit full force till about midnight, so the roads were still dangerous, but passable.

"To cover our alibi, we'll get Moose to confirm it, and that should put us in the clear if anyone claimed they saw us."

"Got it," Jasper pulled into Main Hall's parking lot. "Not that hard to remember."

"Just tell the truth until we left the Muni. Then start the fake story."

Roland lumbered out of the car and made his way into Main Hall, confident in the credibility of their bogus tale.

Later, alone in his work cubicle, his thoughts wormed their way back to Friday night and what really happened.

•   •   •

The Truth

Last Friday night after leaving the Muni, Jasper's car had failed to start. Roland couldn't call Moose and say they'd be late. Shops and gas stations were closed, so no phones available. They decided to walk the eleven blocks to the college, but the blizzard worsened, causing them to stray off course as they dragged themselves up Elmcrest Drive.

When they made it to the high school on 15th Street, they could barely see the red brick building. Roland had heard of farmers tying ropes between their houses and barns so they could find their way back and forth in blizzards like this. He needed a rope all the way to the college now.

"God, I can't breathe," Jasper had yelled over the wind. "We gotta stop. Can't see."

Roland wouldn't admit it, but for the first time in years, terror gripped him. Would they survive this? The wind howled, snowflakes swirled, blinding their eyes. An image of the Wendigo monster of Chippewa lore flashed through his mind. Was the creature lurking in the shadows? The closer you got to him, the colder it got. Every Indian kid knew that. Was he losing his mind?

"Come on," Jasper shouted. "Over here. Found a break from the wind." They hunkered against a wall protected by an enclosure on both sides.

They caught their breath, but Roland knew they must keep moving or they'd freeze.

With back-breaking effort, they continued to stumble north on Elmcrest. Panting. Wheezing. Wiping their dripping noses with scarves and gloves.

Disoriented, Roland hollered, "Let's turn here. Maybe it's a street to the college."

He didn't know how much time had passed, but through the driving snow, he saw a shadow of a hulking figure ahead. Too winded to yell, he saw the hulk bend over something in the snow. Stepping closer, Roland realized the figure was a man in a heavy parka. The guy stood, his hood blowing off. He pulled it up. Was that Albert Melowski? Big college linebacker?

Crap, he didn't want to run into that asshole, not here, not anywhere. He grabbed Jasper, and half-pulled him off the road to hide in the snow drifts in case the guy spotted them, unlikely as it was.

A couple minutes later, Roland grabbed Jasper's sleeve. He managed to blunder along, and they ended up on another road or wide pathway; hard to tell. His eyes watered like a faucet. His nose wouldn't quit running.

Next thing Roland knew, they'd made it to Northland Avenue, crossed, and finally reached the college. It took a while for Moose and the boys to find each other, but the whole night had been a blur for both Roland and Jasper. Moose must've been waiting forever for them.

Cautiously navigating the howling wind and treacherous roads, Moose drove them to his place by the bait shop where they sacked out for the night. By some miracle, the telephone worked, so Jasper called his mother, assuring her he was safe.

The next morning, Moose drove Jasper home and dropped Roland off at Main Hall. Inside, Roland made the trek to his work area where his boss, Charlie, was unpacking a box of lightbulbs. His graying hair hung in his eyes. "Morning, Roland. Hey, heard some bad news this morning."

He told Roland the details of the early-morning discovery of a frozen girl, saying that a neighbor lady had let her dog out to pee at the crack of dawn. The pooch spotted something and wouldn't budge.

Charlie continued. "She about croaked when she saw it. The body of someone half-hidden in a snowbank. Then she called the cops."

Roland felt a knot of dreadful realization rising in his gut.

"They're not releasing her name yet, but I'll tell it to you. It was Dave Gruen's sister, Barbara."

Roland's eyes widened. His heart flew to his throat. "What? Who? You sure?"

Charlie must've noticed Roland's reaction. "Oh God, kid. Did you know her?"

Roland cleared his throat, choked on his words. "Ah … yeah," he stammered. "Knew who she was."

"Nice kid I hear," Charlie said. "But I wasn't supposed to tell anyone the name, so keep it under your hat. Word will get out soon anyway."

Roland nodded, still standing immobile. In a trance.

"By the way, hate to ask you buddy, but can you go to Campus Pantry and buy some snacks for the break room? Ran out of 'em right before the storm." Charlie lit a Chesterfield. "Sidewalks should be passable. Storm's letting up." He handed Roland a wad of cash.

"I'll keep my coat on and go now." The tiny store was several blocks away, easy walking distance from campus. Glad for an excuse to leave, Roland figured the fresh air would help clear his mind. And his stomach. How could the reality sink in?

• • •

Walking back from the store, he'd run into Nancy Borg all bundled up. He wondered if she'd heard the news. They chatted a minute, both shivering. When she headed for her friend's place, Roland thought his head would explode. He wished he could tell someone, but he knew what would happen. Albert would turn the tables on him, wondering how Roland knew. Who would people believe? An Indian?

CHAPTER 16

Nancy
Thursday

I woke up with a dense gloom tugging me down into the sheets. No sunlight swept its way through my meager window, not that I expected morning light yet. Morning light? Maybe next summer if we're lucky.

I inched my way up and stretched, uselessly trying to straighten my back. I thought of the diary and reached under the mattress to retrieve it where I'd safely stashed it from my family's prying eyes. However, who would look under my mattress? No one changed the sheets but me.

As I held the small book, I ran my fingers over its smooth vinyl cover and gently opened the pages for the first time. I didn't need the missing key; it was already unlocked. I thumbed my way along the pages, once again resisting the temptation to read them. How long could I hold out before I discovered Barbara's secret thoughts, goals, desires? Still reluctant to invade her privacy, even though she was gone forever, I carefully hid the diary back in its given spot.

Upstairs, I finished my oatmeal and sipped coffee while I studied my reading assignment for Russian Literature class later this morning. The phone's irritating jangle interrupted my concentration, but at least I was alone for once.

"Hello." I stepped back to the table. "Oh, hi Jude." More bad tidings, no doubt.

Judy sighed deeply. "The cops are clamping down more every day. Now they say Barbara's fractured nose could be caused by smothering, according to the examiner. This is the first time they're declaring foul play."

"My God. I can't believe this." The knot in my stomach tightened. I figured as much, but to have the cops say it out loud was a punch of reality.

Judy's voice cracked. "I know. We're living in the twilight zone. Anyway, more kids have come forward … lots of pressure from the two main cops. The roommate and other girl who took Barbara to the party repeated their story. They didn't see her leave, but saw her talking to a guy at the party, they identified as good old Albert Melowski, drunk on his ass."

"What? Well, he's always been a jerk." I asked myself why Albert would talk to a quiet girl like Barbara.

Judy continued. "Get this. A few other kids thought he was making a pass at her, but she wasn't interested and tried to shove him away. And why would a conceited football champ want to come on to Barbara who's only a sophomore and innocent—"

"He probably thought she was young and cute," I interrupted. "Figured she'd be easy prey. Another notch in his belt." Anger surged through me. "He probably got mad when she rejected him … bruised his ego. He could've followed her—"

"Don't get carried away, but he may have been the reason she left in the blizzard."

"Well, I'm glad he didn't get to first base with her. What an asshole."

"I know," Judy said. "Well, I gotta get ready for our trip tomorrow. Still the same arrangements. You packed yet?"

"Almost." Tomorrow was Barbara's funeral, and I planned to ride with Judy to Grand Rapids. "Wish I could talk Peggy into coming along."

"Me too. Well, I'll be at your house about eight-thirty. Dave plans to leave earlier with his folks. Gotta run. Bye, Nance." Judy hung up.

Later, traipsing my way to the college, I noticed a trace of sunlight trying to flicker through the trees. Mom said the temperature had warmed up to minus eight degrees, so hope was in the air. Snow still clothed the outdoors, silently hiding skeletons and secrets. I didn't hear a sound. Not even a car horn.

Ten minutes later, I sat in my Thursday linguistics class, once again listening to Dr. Maki drone on about who knows what. At last, he gave his horn-rimmed glasses a polish with his handkerchief and bid us a long-awaited farewell. Or in his words, *Hyvasti*. What was so great about the Finns, anyway?

I headed for Peggy's office to have coffee before I went home for lunch.

She looked up from her typewriter as I approached her desk in the admissions office. "How's everything?"

"Okay, I guess." I flopped my jacket and books on a chair across from her desk. "Judy called and said they heard—"

"Yeah, she called me too. Can you believe? Big linebacker Melowski, so full of himself, getting rejected. I'd laugh if it weren't so … so tragic."

I settled on the other chair as Peggy rose and poured two cups from the coffee urn in the corner. She set a scalding mug on the desk by my chair.

We talked further about Judy's latest news, and then I asked, "Any chance you'll change your mind and come with us tomorrow?"

Peggy's lips tightened into a straight line. "Sorry, Nance, I have to work. I don't wanna ask the boss for more time off after my vacation day last week. Even if I could, I have nothing to wear to a funeral."

"Oh, Lord, you don't have to dress up. Just something black or brown or—"

"I don't want to be around Loreen. She'll be dressed to the nines. What would she think?"

I felt my jaw drop. "Peggy Ann Olsen, since when do you care what Loreen thinks? None of us care what she thinks, even Judy, her own daughter."

Peggy's pale eyes glistened with tears. "I know. I know. I just … just drop it will you?"

I'd put my foot in my mouth again. "I'm sorry. I can't think straight these days."

Maybe Peggy's reasons were more deep-seated, but she had claimed her childhood woes were behind her. Besides, she didn't live at home anymore where her old man could whip her and her brothers with a razor strap.

•   •   •

Walking home from Main Hall, my mind strayed to Barbara's parents and the painful arrangements they were forced to make. I imagined them and Dave selecting a casket, choosing Barbara's dress, arranging the funeral service.

I arrived home, and after lunch Judy called again. "Dave and his folks just left for Grand Rapids to tend to final arrangements. Mom and Dad will leave this afternoon and spend the night in a motel. So, we'll meet all of them at the service tomorrow. I don't wanna spend the night, so we can drive back after the funeral." I think Judy needed to talk about humdrum details to take her mind off her painful reality.

I'd asked her how the casket would be transported to Grand Rapids, a three-hour drive southeast.

"Well, Colson Funeral Home is driving the casket there in a van, following the Gruens. They'll leave the body … um, Barbara at the Grand Rapids funeral home for them to take to the church Friday morning. Mrs. Gruen wanted Barbara to travel with them on the road so she wouldn't be alone."

I couldn't fathom the heartbreak of driving three hours to your daughter's final resting place, her body following close behind. I imagined Barbara wanting her hearse to catch up and cry out, *wait for me, wait for me. I'm not ready.*

CHAPTER 17

Loreen
Thursday

Loreen dreaded what tomorrow would bring. She needed to finish packing for the funeral, although she rather looked forward to wearing her new dress. She wanted to drive home late afternoon when everything was over, but Will preferred staying later to help the Gruens handle the mandatory hotdishes, cakes, and other goodies people kindly deliver after a funeral. *We need to offer our support, dear. Their relatives may not make it if the roads are bad. Someone needs to help out besides Dave.*

Loreen had suppressed a groan. How happy she'd be when life would return to normal.

From her bedroom, she heard voices coming from Judy's room. Dave was polishing up his final touches to the eulogy, with Judy gently encouraging him and helping with grammar and sentence structure. Loreen felt sorry for the poor kid paying tribute to his sister who died so young. He was determined to honor Barbara one last time by speaking aloud to the mourners.

Studying her open suitcase on the bed, Loreen wondered what more she needed besides the new dress from O'Brien's. Her black mink wrap would look stunning around her neck. She reached in the closet and fingered the velvety texture, reminding her of Soldier's smooth, floppy ears.

But would the people at the church wonder *who is that lady putting on airs?* After all, Loreen would probably be the only woman in the room who owned a fur wrap. The Gruens weren't exactly the Vanderbilts.

She recognized the meanspirited nature of her thoughts, but stress made her worse than usual, or so she believed.

She returned the mink to the closet and closed the suitcase. Why did she care so much?

Loreen heard tapping at her door, and Judy walked in, her eyes circled in red. "Mom, Dave finished the eulogy, and he and his folks decided on an epitaph for the gravestone. Of course, it'll all take over a month, but they wanted to—"

"I know how difficult this has been, but after time passes, it won't hurt as much." Loreen was at a loss for more words.

Judy sniffled, nodding. She grabbed a Kleenex from the end table. "I can't look at Dave's mom and dad without choking up. They both look so … so broken."

Loreen drew Judy into her arms. "Mom, you always smell so good." They laughed at the absurdity of the comment.

"Thank you, dear. Nothing like the floral aroma and musky undertones of Chanel No. 5, according to the *Vogue* ads, that is," Loreen quoted. "Anyway, we needed a little comic relief."

Judy sat on the bed, drew a piece of folded paper from her shirt pocket, and slowly opened it. "Since Barbara always loved Emily Dickinson, Dave and his folks chose this for the epitaph." She handed it to her mother. "It'll be engraved under her name."

Loreen cautiously reached for the paper as if afraid of it. There, in Judy's careful handwriting, Dickinson's words seemed to speak aloud:

Unable are the Loved to die

For Love is Immortality

Loreen looked at her daughter, clearing her throat. "It's … it's beautiful."

Brushing a tear aside, for the first time in years, Loreen Sandberg felt like two cents waiting for change.

CHAPTER 18

Roland
Saturday

Roland trudged up the steps to Main Hall, deep in thought. A whole week had passed since he'd heard about Barbara. He still felt her spirit surrounding him, almost like the ghost of Sally Roy haunting the edges of his mind.

Overhearing a spattering of vague rumors the past several days, he had no sign that he nor Jasper would be questioned. All he heard was Albert Melowski and his pals were drunk at the party and may have seen Barbara. He'd noticed the cops milling around the campus halls talking to staff members and random students.

So far, so good. Roland's boss had asked him to work overtime this morning to help set up for a two-day conference. At noon his uncle would pick him up, and they'd drive to the reservation where he and Moose would visit Roland's family for a bit.

.   .   .

Three hours later, Roland finally finished arranging tables and chairs. In the hallway, he spotted Dr. Sandberg.

"Good morning, Roland," the professor waved. "Working overtime, I see."

"Yes, sir. Just got done. I'm heading home, since the roads are clear." He couldn't wait to get away from work. "Weather's finally warming up."

The professor's face looked yellowish, haggard. "Yes, this winter's been unusually trying." He stifled a yawn. "I just came in to check my memos. Didn't get much sleep last night. We got home late from Barbara Gruen's funeral. It was in Grand Rapids, you know."

Roland's stomach tightened. He felt flushed. "Oh, yeah." He looked at the floor. "How was … I'll bet …" He stammered, tongue-tied.

"It's okay, son. The service at the family's church was very well-planned and meaningful. Of course, such a painful time. It was good Nancy Borg could come; she rode with Judy."

Still unable to speak, Roland nodded and cleared his throat.

Dr. Sandberg paused as if considering. "This may not be the right time to ask, but have you heard anything new? Anything that could help the investigation? You know, rumors and such that other kids wouldn't …" His voice broke off. "Of course, whatever is said to me would be strictly confidential."

Roland froze. Did Sandberg suspect something? He forced himself to speak. "Um … no sir, I haven't heard. I don't talk much to students, just a few here and there." His instinct kicked in. He stopped himself from mentioning Nancy as an exception. Why muddy the waters?

"Right, I understand," Sandberg turned and waved. "You have a good weekend, Roland. See you Monday."

Practically stumbling down the hall and out the door, Roland felt fear coiling around his chest. Surely no one knew the truth that Roland and Jasper were there that night. Shortly after the party. Seeing Melowski, not realizing until later he was bending over Barbara lying in the snow.

When Roland spotted Moose's car, he headed toward it, almost yanking the door off as he scrambled into the passenger seat.

"In a hurry to leave the trenches?" Moose joked.

"You bet." Roland twisted his parka around and settled in. He stared out the window, trying to relax as they wheeled down 15th Street toward Northland Avenue.

"It's warming up," Moose said. "The snow's thinning out; we may even see some patches of bare earth on the way."

Roland willed himself not to think about Barbara's funeral and Sandberg's comments. He needed to quit worrying. Probably suspicious for no good reason.

They turned right on Northland toward the edge of town, Moose avoiding occasional slick patches on the street. He turned onto Highway 2 heading west. "Any more news on the investigation?"

Roland sure wished people would quit asking that. "Not that I've heard." Was there more to Moose's question than met the eye?

They veered onto Highway 89 and drove north toward the reservation. Roland hoped his uncle would be quiet for a while and leave him alone to ruminate.

His forehead leaning against the window, Roland gazed at the scenery, bleak and desolate, trees barren, lakes and ponds mostly frozen. Occasional dark circles of melted ice appeared on lakes and ponds, promising warmer days ahead.

He forced himself to think of the weekend, bumming around with his cousin and a couple pals who kept their noses clean. That is, clean from crime, booze, and drugs. Moose would hang around with his brother, Roland's pa. They'd smoke pipes or cigars and chew the fat about the good ol' days which weren't all that good.

At least they lived a decent life now. They'd added cheap insulation to the shack after the war, and now everyone in the Nightbird family had a place to sleep.

When Roland was ten years old, their first shack had one room and two beds. Before Ma ran off, she, Pa, and the baby slept in one, and Roland and his two orphan cousins in the other. Three to a bed. Lord, how did they survive the biting cold, dysentery, pneumonia? Not to mention months of frozen ground causing the outhouse to … he shoved that picture out of his mind.

"The town always looks the same," Roland said as they chugged along past a spattering of run-down shacks and several bundled-up men plodding along toward nowhere on the snow-covered road.

When Moose slowed down, the men barely moved to let him pass. He lowered his window a tad. "That you, Ollie? What no good thing have you been up to?"

"Nothin' since yer not around. Gonna stay awhile? See George?"

"Yup. Got his boy with me."

Roland raised his hand in a wave. Ollie bent down, eyed him. "Hey, Roland, they still askin' about the frozen girl in town? I hear it might've been somethin' fishy."

"Don't know any more than you do," Roland lied, anxious to drive off.

"See ya around, Ollie." Moose began rolling up his window. "Don't take any wooden nickels."

"Is Ollie doing better?" Roland asked as they drove off.

"I dunno. Hard to say, his wife dying and his no-good sons running off, gettin' into booze, drugs, robbed a liquor store down in Tenstrike, I hear."

"Guess I was lucky to have you and Pa growing up. And Nani Dinah too." Roland said.

"Nah, you turned out proud on your own, kid. You were born good."

Roland doubted that, but he kept quiet as they passed stick-like shrubs, birches, stray bony dogs. This entire land was a skeleton, voiceless, waiting for better days.

The forlorn façade of St. Catherine's Mission School reminded him of his grammar school days. He could still smell the damp wood and musty hallways. Resembling an old two-story home, there it slumped, like a ragged hobo waiting for a handout.

Driftwood-like logs from forgotten railroad tracks gave mute testimony to the trains that once hauled lumber from the reservation. Folks didn't use timber as much these days.

Moose drove by the village of Thunder Lake, forever tattered and downcast. The white clapboard corner store, once the old General Store, sat next to the post office, an American flag limp above the door.

They passed abandoned-looking trailers, the front yards blemished with broken-down cars on blocks, rusted swing sets waiting for summer. Wooden and concrete shacks varied in size, some more dilapidated than others.

"Eh, home at last." Moose steered his way up the Nightbirds' narrow so-called driveway. Parking behind George's old Ford rust bucket, Moose climbed out of the car. George must've heard them and stepped onto the front concrete porch.

"Get in 'ere, you two, before you freeze 'yer nuts off." He grinned widely, showing tobacco-stained teeth almost matching his brown weathered skin. He had a face like a frying pan and hands resembling boxer mitts.

A familiar smell of tobacco and stale grease hung in the air. George slapped both Moose and Roland on the back. "Come on in, set a spell."

Tossing their parkas onto a chair, they flopped on the frayed sofa, a scorched cigarette hole prominent on the armrest. George, guzzling his own beer, brought them each a can of Hamm's.

"Hey, good to see ya." Roland's grandma Dinah bustled through the back door. "How's my boy? Got a bear hug for your old Gookomis?" Roland stood, put his arms around her ample shoulders. She must've gotten hold of some whiskey.

"She's pretty lonely with your sisters gone, and you just comin' home weekends," George said as Dinah plopped into an easy chair near the sofa.

She smoothed her long gray braids forward on her shoulders. Her faded floral housedress looked like a flour sack. "What's new, Roland? What about that frozen girl? Did you ever see her at work?"

Roland cleared his throat. "No. Didn't know her. No news that I've heard of." Lying came easy for him these days.

Dinah groaned as she stood up. "Damn knees are giving out." She went to the kitchen and returned with a can of beer and a plate of Hydrox chocolate cookies. "Just got these at the store yesterday. Have some, Roland." She set the plate on a TV tray.

Roland took a couple and stuffed one in his mouth. "Ah, thanks."

"What's fer supper, Ma?" George took a swig from his drink.

"You're all in for a real treat." Dinah sat back in her chair, taking a gulp. "I just put the rice and corn on and got the perch ready to fry up. Wesley next door was on the ice today and brought the fish on over. Always a good neighbor."

Roland perked up. He hadn't eaten fresh fish in weeks.

They sat around, drinking, smoking hemp cigarettes, and chatting about neighbors, relatives, and the state of the world.

"Gonna start the fish." Dinah stood with a grunt and carefully walked a straight line to the kitchen.

With her out of earshot, George leaned in and stared at his son with black steely eyes. "Roland, you remember when you started that college job? We was worried if you'd be safe around all them white folks, plus the college kids drink like fish. It would make 'em bolder. So, yer cousin Jesse said he'd get you a knife for protection."

Why bring this up now? Roland glanced toward the kitchen. "Kinda forgot about it, but he did get me one." His eyes studied his feet.

"Yeah, we heard they're trying to outlaw switchblades," said Moose. "Cuz of violence. Inner city gangs and all that."

"Better take good care of it, boy." George eyed Roland. "Whites gettin' restless about it, blaming us for the crimes, of course."

"We gotta do more," Moose said, and he and George continued hashing over the Indians' lot in life.

Roland pretended to listen, but his mind drifted to the four-inch knife buried in his locked cabinet at work. College maintenance workers were given a personal file cabinet drawer with a key. A secure place for wallets, money, and hidden switchblades.

Although no one would guess Roland possessed such a knife, his pa warned him to make sure no white person ever saw it. He always took his pa's advice. Respecting your elders had been drummed into Indian kids since they were knee high to a grasshopper.

However, with a growing sense of foreboding, nothing he could put his finger on, he felt he might need the knife now more than ever.

CHAPTER 19

Nancy
Saturday

Judy and I had arrived home from Barbara's funeral late last night. The next morning, I'd slept until 9:30, leisurely curling under the covers. I forced myself to sit, planted my feet on the cold floor, and stumbled to the bathroom. Visions of Barbara imbedded themselves in my mind.

At least the weather had warmed, with temperatures rising to a balmy five above zero.

Yesterday when Judy had driven out of town toward Grand Rapids, I took in the snow-dusted yards, trees, houses. Same scenery as last October, except smaller snowbanks.

"I'm dreading this more than the memorial service," Judy had said. "I heard from Dave yesterday, and it was tough getting things arranged like flowers, music ..."

"I can't imagine." I twisted in my seat, hoping we wouldn't talk about Barbara anymore. Or talk about anything. I craved silence.

... I am weary of words and people, Sick of the city, wanting the sea, the poet's words, magically expressing my own emotions. Edna St. Vincent Millay hit the nail on the head with that one, even though the sea was over a thousand miles away.

• • •

Still in my bedroom, I recalled yesterday's funeral. I'd managed to sit dry-eyed until Dave's eulogy. He choked up at times, telling memories of Barbara as a little girl. *She'd hide in the hydrangea bush by the front porch, and I'd pretend to look all over until I found her. Then she'd scream and laugh …*

Dave kind of fell apart for a moment, but composed himself and soldiered on.

I squirmed in my seat off and on until the closing hymn. I've always loved the melancholy strains and symbolism of "Be Still, My Soul," Finnish composer Jean Sibelius's iconic "Finlandia."

"They chose the song because Mrs. Gruen is Finnish and has lots of relatives here and in Michigan," Judy explained later. "It's played at all their funerals I was told."

I'd turned into jelly by the time we'd sung the final lines. *Be still, my soul: when change and tears are past, all safe and blessed we shall meet at last.*

I certainly hope so, sweet Barbara. I certainly do.

• • •

I forced myself to stay in the present as I finished dressing, then climbed upstairs for breakfast. The house breathed a welcome silence, and I didn't know or care where the family was.

I bundled up and headed to Peggy's apartment for the usual Saturday gossip, coffee, and if we were lucky, homemade cinnamon rolls. Judy would join us, since Dave was still in Grand Rapids helping his folks complete the customary paperwork and other post-funeral tasks.

Peggy looked wafer-thin as she opened the door. Her gray sweater hung on her as if draped over a coatrack. "Finally warmed up."

I almost asked if she was okay, but restrained myself. "Yeah, what a relief. I can wear lightweight sweaters again."

We sat at her kitchen table drinking coffee and puffing away on our Winstons. Peggy seemed restrained, like something had shifted in her. I couldn't put my finger on it. I folded my napkin in two and smoothed down the crease.

"Do you want to hear more about the funeral?" I asked tentatively.

"Sure." She nodded, her voice flat.

"The service was so well-done. Sad, of course, but really touching."

"Umm," Peggy murmured, then sucked in her cigarette, her lips pursed.

I continued rattling on, unsure if she was bored, hurt, or what. Hell, I'm not a mind-reader.

"The music really got to me," I continued. "A male soloist, baritone I think, sang "How Great Thou Art." After a while, we all sang "Abide With Me" and at the end, "Be Still My Soul.""

Peggy's eyes glistened. "Yeah, that would've done me in too, especially the last hymn. A real tear-jerker."

"And the minister also quoted the epitaph that'll be on the gravestone. The lines from Emily Dickinson, *Unable are the Loved to die, For Love is Immortality*."

I sipped my coffee. "I wonder where Barbara is now. Can her spirit see us? Or only those who ... who loved her?"

Peggy shrugged. "I don't know, Nance. No one does. But plenty of people believe in heaven."

The ding-dong of the doorbell interrupted our words. I heard Judy's voice as Peggy opened the door. "Is Nancy here already?"

After Judy settled herself with a cigarette and coffee, she sighed. "Oh Lord, why can't all this be over so poor Barbara can rest in peace?"

No one answered.

Judy exhaled. Ringlets of smoke sailed upward and like everything beautiful, they disappeared. "Latest news is a witness who says he saw Albert Melowski leave the party after Barbara."

Peggy and I talked at once; I shut up and let her speak.

"You mean Albert followed Barbara out when she left the party?"

Judy hesitated. "Could be. I'm not sure he actually saw her leave, but probably. Anyway, Albert left and the witness snuck out after him. He said Al just crept down the block doing nothing. Just huddling around."

"Who was the witness?" I shivered, suddenly cold.

Judy lowered her voice as if other people were in the room. "Dad said it's this Earl guy. Forget the last name. He told the cops he insisted on staying anonymous. They promised, unless things go south and he himself is suspected of something ... or whatever." Judy lit another cigarette and took a drag. Her auburn hair curtained her oval face and clear skin. Why couldn't I be pretty?

I joined Judy in another Winston. One of these days, I'd quit. Yeah, right. "I think I know that Earl guy. Might not be in Albert's inner circle, but they're in the same group of football morons."

Peggy poured us more coffee and set a plate of Nabisco ginger snaps on the table. "Oh, I know Earl ... Earl Krepp. He's okay, nice enough, kind of quiet. He's been in the office for job recruitment applications."

Judy crunched a bite of cookie. "Remember, Dad said this info is confidential, but he knows damn well it won't be for long. Anyway, I can't possibly keep secrets from you two." She smiled for the first time that morning.

I pushed my chair back, stood, and tried to straighten my back. Dang thing was aching again.

"What's the next step?" I asked Judy. "I wonder if the cops will go public pretty soon with Melowski as a suspect. Guess they won't blab Earl's name, since they promised they wouldn't."

"Dad didn't say what the cops will do next. But there's a reporter from the newspaper nosing around the police station, asking about suspects, and what progress has been made."

We sat, as if deep in thought.

Judy crushed her cigarette out in the growing pile of ashes and butts. Peggy needed to empty the ashtray more often, but I wasn't about to suggest it.

"I'll tell you one thing." Judy's eyes flared at us like a frightened horse. "If that asshole Albert killed Barbara, well, I won't say what I'd like to do."

I thought it best to keep my mouth shut.

CHAPTER 20

Loreen
Monday

Loreen pretended not to hear the muffled sounds of Will stretching, tugging the sheets around himself one last time before climbing out of bed. But she deserved to sleep late after the past week of unrest, anxiety, a funeral, and people annoying her like ants at a picnic.

An hour later, dawn filtered its way through the bedroom drapes. Loreen turned over and leaned against the pillow, fortifying herself for another fruitless day.

Soldier trotted through the door.

"Hi, buddy," she said. "What's in store for us today?" She leaned down and nuzzled the spaniel's silky neck and satin ears. "Do you smell like cold damp fur from your morning potty time?" Soldier licked her cheek in response.

Following Loreen into the bathroom, the dog sat and watched her with somber brown eyes.

She splashed cold water on her face, dried off, and studied herself in the mirror. "Oh Lord." She parted her henna hair, examining recent strands of silver mocking her vanity.

She'd need to make an appointment at her beauty shop today. After all, her hair was not permitted to turn gray.

Several minutes later at breakfast, Loreen pondered her wardrobe. No plans for today, other than shopping at O'Brien's if nothing else came up. Alma said she might stop in for coffee if she had time. Loreen decided on her blue and white Icelandic sweater with navy pants to be on the safe side. She had to look nice if Alma showed up, not to mention the clerks at O'Brien's.

• • •

At lunch time, Alma hadn't come over. Loreen sighed and took a small frying pan from the cupboard to prepare grilled cheese sandwiches for Will's lunch. He soon bustled through the door and petted Soldier on the head.

"Ready to go out, boy?" Will turned back outside, the pooch happily scampering behind.

Several minutes later, Will joined Loreen in the kitchen where they sat down to eat. After ten minutes of idle conversation, Will swallowed a bite of sandwich and finished his glass of milk. "Nothing new on the investigation this morning. They're still saying Barbara died of asphyxiation rather than hypothermia. Because of where the damaged—"

"Do we have to talk about it at the table? How am I supposed to eat hearing about broken parts on a dead girl's body? Why can't they let sleeping dogs lie?" Loreen plunked her silverware down. "Let it go already."

Will's eyebrows shot upward. "You really feel that way? If someone killed her you don't care if he's punished or just goes free to do it again?"

"I didn't mean that. I've just been in a dither since Barbara's …" Loreen felt a hint of shame.

Will stared at her as if for the first time. "We all know you'd never be mistaken for Harriet Nelson, but really."

Ouch! That hurt. Momentarily Loreen, defenses up, huffed and shoved her chair back. "For your information, I don't watch

Ozzie and Harriet, so I don't know who you're talking about," she fibbed. "You can clear the table. I have a headache. Need a nap."

With that, she marched upstairs to take a well-earned rest atop her silken sky-blue bedspread. She needed to lick her wounds. Will's comment cut her to the quick.

After a few minutes, she sat up and slinked downstairs. She didn't want Will to return to work angry with her. She wasn't that horrible a wife. Halfway down the stairs, the phone jangled.

The ringing stopped. Then Will's muffled voice. She tiptoed the final steps and softly treaded to his office near the living room. The door was ajar, allowing her to lean in and eavesdrop.

"Why, that's preposterous." Will's voice rose an octave. "We can't believe rumors."

Pause. "No, I think that's a bad idea. We won't accuse anyone of anything until there's more evidence. Roland has an excellent record. He's well-liked around campus."

Another pause. "No, Jack, I won't be involved. Just because someone heard it through the grapevine doesn't—"

Silence. "I gotta go. See you later." Before Will slammed down the receiver, Loreen scurried toward the stairs.

"What are you doing there?" Loreen thought she was safe, but Will hadn't lingered in the office. "I thought you were going up to nap."

Loreen wondered if she looked as guilty as she felt. But she couldn't help herself. "Will, I heard you on the phone and—"

"You were listening in?" A frown creased his forehead. "Really, Loreen—"

"Honey, you know me. What's this about the Indian kid? Is he accused of something? Something about Barbara?"

"It's just hearsay." He seemed to consider whether to keep talking. "Well, a kid told the cop that he'd heard, mind you, just heard that Roland was around the place where Barbara was found."

"Aha," Loreen nodded emphatically. "I knew an Indian had something to do with it. So they're picking on that Albert kid and ignoring the most obvious—"

"Loreen." Will's voice rose a decibel or two. "Stop! I won't have that kind of talk in this house. And this is strictly confidential. You weren't supposed to know any of this. And don't you dare tell Judy or Dave."

Shocked, Loreen stepped backward. She'd never heard Will yell at her like that. She felt her cheeks flush. Afraid or angry? What was she?

They stood, staring at each other. "What is this?" Loreen asked. "Custer's last stand?"

"Not funny, Loreen. You may not realize Custer didn't—"

"Who gives a damn? You and your eternal sympathy for the Indians. Always on their side."

Loreen spun around and once again, stomped up the stairs. She hoped she could resist the temptation to tell Judy. But then again, maybe her daughter would be on her side.

CHAPTER 21

Roland
Wednesday

For the past couple days at work, Roland's mental radar had been on high alert. The atmosphere had shifted, his boss seemed distant, guys he worked with didn't look him in the eye. He tried to convince himself it was his imagination. But then, even his pa and Moose had mentioned the investigation last weekend on the reservation.

Around noon, Roland had glimpsed a couple cops down the hall. Damn, what were they doing here? Still questioning students and staff about Barbara?

He unlocked his cabinet drawer and fished around for his brown bag lunch of one banana, a baloney sandwich, and several Hydrox vanilla cookies. He hadn't brought a drink in his bag and didn't want to buy one at the canteen, so he lay low in his chair and unwrapped his food. He thought of his switchblade buried under a pair of gloves in the drawer.

"There you are," said Will Sandberg.

Startled, Roland held his sandwich midair without taking a bite. His heart hammered against his ribs. "Hello, Dr. Sandberg. Just having my lunch … as you can see." He forced a smile.

"Listen Roland, if you could come to my office in a few minutes … you finish your lunch first, no hurry."

Sandberg must have noted the confused look on Roland's face, edged with wariness. "The police may have more information about Barbara's death, but nothing definite, so it's okay. They're talking to more staff, and your maintenance crew is included."

Roland coughed. Looked at his un-bitten sandwich. "Uh, okay, sure. Should I just come and knock on your door when I'm done eating?"

"That would be fine." Sandberg inched his way toward the hall. "Don't worry, it's just routine. You know how these things go." He waved a casual goodbye and hurriedly left the room.

Roland took a nibble of his sandwich and choked it down. Tasted like cardboard. Thinking he could stomach a banana, he forced it halfway down, then tossed the rest in the trash. He even left the cookies untouched.

Crap, was this the end for him? People had it in for Indians. Everyone knew that. He wished he could remember the old Chippewa prayer to the Great Spirit or whoever they believed in these days. His grandfather, One Arrow, used to chant the prayer during times of struggle, pretty much all the time.

He took two deep breaths and made his feet plod toward Sandberg's office. Another guy in the maintenance group was just leaving, closing the office door.

"Hey, buddy. You up next?"

Confused, Roland answered. "Up next?"

The guy laughed. "You know, the firing squad. Don't worry, they won't scalp ya." Still guffawing at his own wit, he strolled away.

Roland tried to swallow, but felt his Adam's apple choking him. Determined not to be a pansy ass, he tapped on the door.

"Come in," called Sandberg.

Roland stepped in the room, which displayed bookshelves on two walls, a large, shiny wood desk, and several waiting chairs with hard seats.

Two uniformed cops occupied chairs across from Sandberg's desk. One man was thin and young, the other an aging boulder of a guy with a face the size of a dinner plate.

"Roland, these are officers Nysen and Bergstrom." The older man, Bergstrom, his pinprick eyes lost in puffy cheeks, nodded at Roland.

Sandberg sat at his desk. "Have a seat, son." He pointed to an empty chair alongside the others.

Nysen, the skinny cop, began. "As you know, Roland, we've been questioning more folks about Barbara Gruen's death. Dr. Sandberg told us you didn't overhear any students or staff talking about the incident that Friday night, but we're just checking up on—"

"Yeah," Bergstrom interrupted, his handlebar mustache twitching. "Maybe you remember something … something that didn't seem important at the time?"

Roland felt everyone's eyes probing through him. "Um, no sir. I don't think so. I mean, not that I can …" He tried to quit stammering.

"You don't think so? You're not sure?" Bergstrom's voice gruff.

"Well, ah, no. I mean, yes." A spark of anger flicked in Roland. Typical cop. Pick on the Indian.

Sandberg gave a quick cough. "I'm sure Roland has heard nothing, Officer. Now, if you don't mind—"

"Say," Bergstrom leaned his sizeable anatomy toward Roland. "You happen to be related to an Eddie Nightbird? A few years ago now …" The cop glanced at Sandberg and shut up.

Roland gulped, fear mingling with anger. He swallowed to buy some time. "He's a second cousin or something; not sure." He wiped a thin layer of sweat from his brow. That loser, Eddie, had gotten into trouble; hauled into the cop station for shoplifting at Woolworth's. That was the story, but Roland heard the offense was more serious.

Sandberg stood, indicating the meeting was over. "Thanks for coming in, Roland. We'll see you tomorrow."

Roland nodded to the cops and left the room, relieved to get the hell out of there. At least the cops had other guys to question. Otherwise, the Bergstrom jerk may follow him out, grilling him about Eddie and what he was up to these days. Roland would've faked ignorance, knowing full well his dumbass cousin continued to be in and out of trouble.

As he shuffled down the hall to his work area, he reminded himself to call Jasper tonight and tell him about the cops' questions. Jasper would ask what they should do, but there was nothing. Keeping quiet was the only way.

But that didn't stop the stomach-churning dread that gripped him.

CHAPTER 22

Roland
Friday . . . Two days later

Roland was sure the ax was ready to fall when Dr. Sandberg once again appeared at the maintenance area mid-morning. "Hello, Roland. I'm afraid you need to come to my office one more time."

"Oh." Roland feigned nonchalance. "All right. Should I come now?"

The professor appeared uneasy. Roland felt the same way; did Sandberg notice his left eye quivering?

"Please," Sandberg turned toward the hallway.

As they walked, Roland felt like a prisoner ready to face a hanging judge. Entering Sandberg's office, Roland was surprised to see Hal Miles of the BIA waiting for them.

Miles held out his hand. "Good morning, Roland. Haven't seen you for how long? A couple years now."

"I guess so." Roland shook hands.

Sandberg said, "Hal is joining us in the questioning this time. We think it will be helpful, so the officers don't take advantage."

Roland understood immediately that Sandberg and Miles were protecting him so the cops wouldn't intimidate the Indian kid. His nerves jangled warning bells.

As if on cue, someone rapped on the door. "Come in," Sandberg said.

Bergstrom, the barrel-sized cop and his cohort entered, gave perfunctory nods, and mumbled greetings to everyone.

Sandberg indicated chairs for the officers. "I know you'll make this as quick as possible, so I'll let you two explain to Roland why he's here." The professor looked none too happy.

Nysen loosened his wool scarf. "Well, Roland, I'll get right to the point. A witness stated he saw a second person in the area where Barbara Gruen was found. This was after she left the party, following the first person who was seen."

The heavyweight leaned forward. "Thing is, Roland, this new guy showed up for a minute after Al … I mean the other person wandered away. This guy was bending over the place where the girl was laying." The cop's eyes drilled a hole through him.

"What's that got to do with me, unless—"

"Unless what, Roland? Unless the second person was you?" Bergstrom tugged the end of his mustache.

"Now just a minute here." Miles straightened in his chair. "You can't go around accusing Roland of anything without proof."

Sandberg cleared his throat and straightened his glasses. "Nysen, just tell us why Roland's here."

Roland felt the room turn warm and stifling. Was he sweating? He readied himself for more bad news.

"Okay," the short cop said. "Thing is, Roland, our witness said even though it was dark outside in blizzard conditions, he barely could make out a silhouette of a big guy creeping out from somewhere and bending over where the Gruen girl was."

There it was, the hangman's noose tightening around Roland's neck.

"Wait," Miles said. "There's gotta be umpteen big guys from that party. How could the so-called witness tell—"

"Because," Bergstrom's voice defiant, "the scarf the guy wore was extra long and trailed out behind his neck." He stared at Roland. "We've heard that Roland here wears a long scarf without fringe, and ties it behind his neck."

Roland felt like a cornered rat. His great aunt Donella had knit the scarf for him two years ago. *Here, Roland, I put red and green tribal patterns on the edges, and it's extra long. It'll bring you good health and happiness.*

The colors didn't scream for attention, and Roland was proud to wear it. Until now.

"And no other guys wear long scarves?" Miles glared at Bergstrom.

After pausing a few seconds, Roland stammered, "I wasn't anywhere near there. I told you before when you asked people in the hallways that I was leaving—"

"I know. I know. You were leaving the Muni." Bergstrom interrupted. "But can you prove exactly where you were and what time it was?"

"And can you, officer, prove that Roland was where you say he was?" Sandberg's voice was gravely.

"We do have our witness." Nysen took out a notepad.

"Who? Who is it?" Roland felt steam rising in his blood.

"I think we're going around in circles here," Sandberg said. "There's clearly no hard evidence that Roland was there."

"That's right," Miles chimed in. "I know enough about the law that Roland doesn't need to be on the witness stand defending himself unless he's been arrested and accused of a crime."

Miles laid his hand on Roland's shoulder. "Don't worry, son. Doesn't seem they have a shred of proof, and the witness's opinion of who's who at midnight in a blizzard based on the shadow of a long scarf is pure horseshit."

Roland felt slightly relieved with two smart men on his side. He probably wouldn't need Moose to cover for him. But when he reached Moose at the college that night, he'd been expecting Roland sooner. A long time unaccounted for. A bothersome dilemma.

He thought of Jasper. The witness had only seen Roland. He'd keep his pal out of it for now. But he'd still need to high tail it and tell Jasper about the rumors that would start up. This was a small town after all. Everyone knew Eklund was a hotbed for gossip.

CHAPTER 23

Nancy
Saturday

Another dreary, morose dawn promised a bleak day ahead. It was Saturday, thank God. I allowed myself to sleep in.

Late last night I'd taken Barbara's diary from its hiding place and opened it. Determined to read only the first page, I cautiously glanced down. I saw the handwritten word, *Journal,* and underneath, *Barbara G., September, 1954--*

How sad. The empty space after the date would forever remain blank. Then I figured the title page didn't count as a real page … not really. So, I turned to the next one and read: *I've been back for my sophomore year for a week, and things are about the same as last year. I haven't seen Him yet, but I'm hoping to —* I slammed the book closed as though Barbara's ghost hovered over my shoulder. Suddenly, I couldn't bear to read more. Let the poor girl have her privacy. Even in death, she deserved it.

I'd realized I could never share the diary with Barbara's family or anyone else. Too late now. I still justified my choice to hide it as impulsive, but ultimately for the best. If I'd kept a journal, would I want it read if someone discovered it, and I was … well, gone? A private account of one's thoughts could hurt loved ones if a painful truth were revealed. Yet, could it help the police? I had to live with my decision.

I hadn't heard updates on Barbara's investigation for days, and life felt dull, an uneasiness skirting around the framework. Eager for my usual Saturday coffee with Peggy, I wolfed down my Wheaties and toast with freshly squeezed orange juice. I'd still have room for cookies or rolls that Peggy often had on hand.

On my way out, Dad griped about a newscast on TV. "More protesting that schools aren't following Brown versus Board of Education." He looked up at me. "Mark my words, Nance, the court never should've passed it. I wouldn't want my kids going to school with—"

"I know. I know." Of course, he was too pig-headed for me to bother debating the subject. People like him never change. Eager to leave him behind, I scurried out the door.

• • •

I breathed a sigh of relief to arrive at Peggy's apartment, sit at her kitchen table, and sip hot coffee.

"Is it any warmer out?" Peggy's gaunt look disturbed me.

"I think it's a sultry twelve degrees above zero. Spring is here!"

Peggy stood at the counter putting peanut chocolate cookies on an aqua Melmac plate. "I baked these last night. Have some." She placed the cookies on the table.

I tried not to be grabby. "Um, delicious. You're a good cook, Peg."

She smiled wanly and drank her coffee, ignoring the cookies.

"Are things okay? Sorry to pry, but you look so thin." Lately, I've felt uncomfortable with her, not knowing what will set her off.

She stared into her coffee cup as if something fascinating were going on in there. "Yeah, I have lost some weight. I haven't had much appetite the past few months." She paused and took another drink.

I nodded. "Maybe you should—"

"I know," Peggy interrupted. "I saw Dr. Norberg, and he couldn't find anything wrong. He said it may be stress, so he gave me Miltown pills."

I'd heard of them, and thought they were tranquilizers. "Are they not helping?"

Peggy's eyes turned wet. "Not really. They make me relaxed, but then I get drowsy in the afternoons."

"Sure wish I could help, but ..." my voice slipped away.

"I know," Peggy spoke softly. "I appreciate that, but let's talk about something else like the latest in the case. Did you talk to Judy last night?"

"No," I said, feeling left out. "What did she say?"

"Well, the Earl Krepp guy says he witnessed another person after Albert left. This new guy supposedly nosed around where Barbara was found and stumbled away. Guess who he thinks it was?"

"I have no idea." I hate guessing games.

"Roland Nightbird. Can you believe it?" Peggy finally reached for a cookie.

I was shocked. "No kidding? It must be a ridiculous rumor. How did Earl identify someone in the blizzard in the middle of the night?"

Peggy retrieved the coffee pot and refilled our cups. "Something about a long scarf he always wore tied in the back of his neck. It was blowing, and everyone knows Roland wears that extra long scarf."

"That's a flimsy reason. I'm sure lots of guys have extra long scarves. Well, some maybe." I couldn't believe Roland would harm anyone. "Besides, didn't he stay with his uncle during the week?"

"Yeah, that's what he told you that time you—"

"That time I ran into him the morning they'd discovered the body?" I tried to recall exactly what he'd said. "I asked what he was doing out in the cold on a Saturday. He said he'd stayed with his uncle because roads were closed to the reservation, and he couldn't get home."

I remembered later, at Peggy's, place, speculating on and on about the poor frozen girl's identity.

Peggy's mouth curved downward. "Yes, seems like ages ago, but it was only … um, two weeks?"

I nodded. "And look how our lives have changed. Especially for Dave and his family."

We finished our coffee, and I devoured a couple more cookies. "Poor Roland. The rumors will be flying. Word leaks out you know; can't stop wagging tongues."

"Peggy added, "It's a good thing he has Will Sandberg and the BIA guy on his side. They got him his job in the first place and have always liked him."

"Lucky for him"

But would that be enough to protect Roland from a possible firestorm?

CHAPTER 24

Loreen
Sunday

"Something the matter, dear?" After dinner, Loreen sensed Will's agitation as he sat in his easy chair reading the *Eklund Daily Post*. He'd been grunting and groaning when she came in the living room.

"I can't believe the audacity of the paper letting this so-called reporter spew out this ridiculous, venomous garbage." He folded the paper.

"Let me see it," Loreen demanded, in no mood to play nice.

"I'm not sure, dear. It may not interest you."

"Will Sandberg, when have you ever lied to me? You're hiding something." She reached for the paper.

Defeated, Will handed it over. "I don't want to hear your opinion unless it's fair."

"For Lord's sake, don't be so melodramatic." She sat in the adjoining chair and unfolded the paper. "Where do I find it?"

"On the editorial page," Will grumbled.

"Yes, it must be the column about life on Thunder Lake Reservation."

Will remained silent and puffed on a cigarette while Loreen perused the article.

Several minutes later, she looked up. "You don't want to hear this, dear, but I'm afraid I kind of go along with the man."

"Somehow, I'm not surprised, but we'll save that discussion for later."

A fair article, in Loreen's opinion. The writer described a couple tumbledown tarpaper shacks with raggedy kids hanging around, chasing dogs and cats, swatting flies. Among other opinions, he mentioned that despite government resources, the Indians have no ambition to better themselves, and most will not succeed in life.

Loreen reached for a pack of Salems on the end table, tapped one out, and lit up. Relieved Will didn't want to debate the Indian editorial, she inhaled deeply and exhaled. A silver stream of smoke moseyed its way toward the ceiling.

Suddenly the door burst open, and Judy and Dave charged inside. "Brrr, it's getting colder out there." Judy's cheeks, the color of cranberries. Soldier yelped his greeting and jumped up on Dave's knees.

"Hi, kids." Will took the newspaper back from Loreen.

"Dad." Judy's voice breathless. "Can you believe the rumors about Roland are flying around already? Pretty soon they'll be all over town."

"What did you expect, dear?" Lorene wore a smug look. "He just may be guilty."

Will and Dave both burst out at once. "You go ahead, Dave," Will said.

"With all due respect, I don't think it's fair to judge anyone until you have proof," Dave said. "After all, our legal system is based on 'innocent until proven guilty,' and I—"

"Excuse me," Loreen spouted, "but I don't need a lecture on our country's judicial system from you or anyone else. You have your opinions. I have mine." Loreen crushed her cigarette into the ashtray with a vengeance.

Will leaned forward. "In Dave's defense, we shouldn't judge someone on rumors, difficult as that is for people in this town."

"But there is pretty good evidence that Roland was there right after Albert left," Judy piped up.

Surprised that everyone wasn't ganging up on her, Loreen said, "Thank you, Judy. That witness could probably be right."

"Right on what?" Dave asked. "Roland's the only kid who has a long scarf?"

"Yeah, one with Indian symbols on it." Judy glared at Dave.

"It was midnight out in a blizzard. How could anyone see symbols on—"

"All right. All right." Will was plainly exasperated. "This argument is going nowhere, and won't be resolved until further information comes out. I'm going to catch up on my paperwork, and I suggest the rest of you do something else other than … other than talk this subject to death." He waved his hand dismissively and retreated to his office.

Loreen stared after him. "Well, I never. I need a drink." She stood and made her way to the liquor cabinet by the dining room, glancing back at Judy.

"By the way, you may be interested in an article in the paper. It's on the editorial page. Now you two try and have a nice evening. I'm going upstairs to drink and read."

Judy shrugged her shoulders and sat down on the sofa next to Dave. "We'll read the article and let you know if you're right or not."

"Mother's always right." Loreen mixed a Manhattan with her favorite Kentucky bourbon and climbed the stairs, Soldier at her heels. She craved a quiet refuge from the unrest of life.

After kicking off her shoes, she reclined on her chez longue, drink in hand, book on her lap. As if to complete a Norman Rockwell picture of family harmony, Soldier turned two times in a circle and flopped down by Loreen's feet.

"You'll always care about me, won't you boy?" She leaned forward and massaged his furry, caramel-colored head.

Three weeks ago, her life was stable. Not happy, really, but stable. Now, her foundation had shifted. The foundation of her family.

CHAPTER 25

Roland
Monday

Roland dreaded showing up for work Monday morning. His gut screamed that rumors would fly all over campus about his presence at the crime scene. He still could not believe a witness had seen him where Barbara's body had been. He'd already heard about Albert being seen too, but he was a white college kid.

He remembered calling Jasper on Friday after work, saying his head was almost on the chopping block. *I know that's exaggerating, but the cops basically accused me of being at the scene right after Albert.*

Aware that Jasper had worried about his own involvement, Roland assured him he would not tell a soul Jasper had been hiding in the snowy shadows.

Spending the weekend at home on Thunder Lake had helped Roland escape his problems for a couple days. He and his father, George, hunted pheasants near the marshlands where the birds would hide in the winter. Roland shot two, which they brought home to Grandma Dinah. *Good job, kid. I'll cook em' up for supper.*

And cook em' up she did, atop her faithful wood-burning cookstove she'd used for decades. In her trusty cast-iron skillet, she'd heated the oil and fried the pheasant parts, adding the usual spices. Then Dinah squeezed lemon juice over everything, her special touch.

Yes, Roland felt lucky to have his family, even if some were black sheep. Mainly him.

• • •

Now, as he plodded down the hall toward his work area, three students cast sidelong glances at him. He wondered how his co-workers would react. And what about Charlie? He should brace himself in case his boss fires him.

"Mornin' Roland," Charlie greeted him. "Step in a minute." He waved toward his cubby hole of an office. The guy wasn't wasting any time.

"Take off your jacket and have a seat." Charlie lowered his bulky frame into his desk chair.

Roland pulled off his gray parka and held it as he sat across from the boss. He studied the well-worn scarf he kept hidden under his coat, its red and green turtle designs made by his great aunt's hands. He'd keep it forever, but it may be good to borrow a scarf from Moose until things blew over.

"Roland, I won't beat around the bush. It's a damn shame the rumors are out about your so-called suspicious doings." He shifted in his chair. "I don't believe a word of it myself, but some idiot kids seem to."

Roland shook his head. "I can't believe this is happening. I've never been in trouble—"

"I know you haven't, son," Charlie interrupted. "Doc Sandberg and the BIA guy, Miles, stopped in late Friday and we talked. Of course, they knew my high opinion of you and your excellent record. We'll vouch for you, no question."

"Thanks a lot. Sure appreciate that." Roland longed for one of Charlie's cigarettes. "What should I do? Take some time off?"

"We thought it best we just go on as usual." Charlie puffed away. "If you left for a few days, it could send the message that we might be suspicious and are covering something up."

Roland nodded in agreement. "I'll just keep my nose to the grindstone and try and look as normal as I can."

• • •

By lunch time, Roland felt slightly more relaxed. He'd stayed in the maintenance area helping Charlie with paperwork and other tasks that kept him from working in other parts of the building, an unspoken arrangement between him and his boss to avoid drawing attention.

The other maintenance guys acted as usual, but Roland wondered what they really knew or thought about the lone Indian in their midst.

Will Sandberg stopped by in the afternoon and took Charlie and Roland aside. "Can we talk in your office?"

Roland felt the air go out of him. More bad news coming. He and Sandberg settled around Charlie's desk. This was becoming routine.

Pouches hung under Sandberg's eyes. He gave a thin, weary smile. "I just wanted to update you two. Rumors are coming to light that someone followed Barbara after the party and was seen shortly before you supposedly were, Roland."

Confused, Roland thought the witness must've blabbed about Albert too. "Really? Well, that's strange." He could think of nothing else to say.

"To be honest," Charlie said, "I'd heard about the other guy, but didn't say anything."

"The man in question is Albert Melowski, which you've probably heard already. Some partygoers finally mentioned that Al was trying to flirt with Barbara." Will's jaw clenched as if he believed Albert was truly guilty of something. Which he was, in Roland's opinion.

Silence filled the room. Finally, Sandberg said, "I can't divulge the witness's name, but I'm sure it'll get out sometime." He stood to indicate the meeting was over. "Just remember, Roland, whatever you hear, do not comment. If any snide remarks come your way, just keep going. The most powerful thing you can do is ignore the bullies and jerks. They feed off getting a rise out of their targets."

Roland could second that advice. How he was brought up. Street smarts. Harder for some folks to ignore their tormenters, but not for him. He'd survive this crisis one way or another.

CHAPTER 26

Nancy
Wednesday

The days crawled by with nothing remarkable happening in my life, including updates on the investigation. But I felt something in the air around campus. Something ominous. Foreboding. I couldn't pinpoint it.

Rumors of Roland's presence the night of the party had spread like weeds.

Yesterday, a chubby blond kid in my education class told me, "Sure is weird the Indian guy was there hanging around that night. He had no business at a college party."

Irritated, I said, "We don't know that, and besides, seems that nobody else had any business where Barbara died. If someone was, why didn't he bother to report it?" I tried to ignore ignorant remarks, but I was fed up with people siding against Roland.

"It seems pretty clear the Indian was there." The kid opened his textbook like he actually read the damn thing.

Anger surged through my veins. "You don't know the facts. Besides, what about big shot Albert? You think he was there? Kids from the party told the cops they saw him, not Roland, flirting with Barbara. Yes, Roland is his name. Anyway, what about Albert?" I paused. "Oh yeah, I forgot. He's a white college kid. A football star to boot." I shoved back my chair and stood.

"By the way," I leaned in for one last word, my voice rising. "How would you feel if you were blamed for something cuz you're a dumb Norski?"

Red-faced, I clambered my way to the back row and sat, students staring in my wake. I felt slightly guilty calling the Norwegian kid a Norski, but I'd been called a dimwitted Swede. All's fair, right?

Inwardly, I seethed through the professor's entire lecture and then high tailed it out the of room toward Peggy's office. Turning a corner down the hall, I ran into Roland. Actually, I'd been wanting to talk to him.

"Hi, Roland. Good to see you." A couple other kids passed us, gawking.

"How do, Nancy. Sure you want to be seen with me?" Roland's marble eyes glanced around.

"I never bother with jerks. Hope you don't either." Easy for me to say. I felt awkward, but wanted to go on. "I … uh, just wanted to say that I don't believe the stupid rumors, and some very smart people are standing by you."

Roland cleared his throat and brushed his black, straight hair from his eyes. He balanced his contractors' broom and long-handled dustpan. "Nice of you to say. Yeah, just gotta ignore 'em."

I sure felt sorry for the guy. So unfair, just because of his dark skin. "I know Dr. Sandberg and other people as well, are on your side." I hitched up my book bag. "Well, I'm gonna go meet Peg. See ya." I gave Roland a warm smile, which I don't bother to give most people.

"Thanks again, Nancy." Roland continued sweeping the hallway, trying to stay out of the way. Far be it from students to sidestep Roland at his menial task.

I wasn't in the mood to see Peggy, but knew she'd wonder why I didn't show up for regular coffee time. However, I was curious if she'd heard anything new from Judy, who hadn't called me lately.

When I reached her desk, Peggy was filing a stack of papers. "Hey, time for a break," I said, setting down my bag and jacket.

"Let's have coffee." She stood, straightening her wool skirt. "I'm sick of these files. Worst part of the job."

From the table I grabbed a green mug emblazoned with "Go Beavers," indicating the college mascot. Peggy poured us piping hot coffee as we sat at her desk. I took in her appearance.

"Looks like you've put on a pound or two. Good for you."

Peggy gave a wan smile. "I've upped my calories lately. I think the Miltown pills help. I'm definitely more relaxed. You should try them."

"Why, aren't I relaxed enough?" I said, thinking of this morning and the Norwegian guy. I'd over-reacted; he was just young and ignorant.

"You? Relaxed? Well, maybe at times," Peggy said. "But let's just say you get shook every now and then."

I wasn't about to belabor the point. "Heard any new gossip lately?"

"More about poor Roland. What's gonna happen to him? Even though he's not guilty of anything, the rumors might do him in."

"I know. I ran into him earlier and said I was on his side, along with some other people."

"The thing is, Nance, it doesn't seem to bother most of the jerks that kids actually saw Al bothering Barbara that night. Being white gives you a pass, doesn't it?"

I didn't answer. Peggy and I sipped our coffee, both of us quiet.

• • •

Later at home, I worked on a Melville composition in my bedroom. When I finished, I climbed up the basement stairs to watch the news. Dad was home early, so I found myself alone with him in the living room. Not a comfortable scene. He sat imbibing his second Jim Beam and reading a newspaper, waiting for Douglas Edwards and the evening news.

"What's this I hear about an Indian kid being questioned for being at the frozen girl's crime scene?"

"What are you talking about?" I sat down with a glass of rum and Coke, my drink of choice these days. Surprised he'd heard the rumors, I asked. "Where did you hear such a thing?" I took a healthy swig.

"Don't play dumb, Nance. It's practically all over town, not just at your hoity-toity college."

I suppose that shouldn't have been a shock. This town got smaller and nosier by the day. "Well, you should know not to believe every hairbrained rumor you hear. You're not a kid, you know."

"Don't get smart. I've been around the block a few times. I know more than you think." He gulped his drink and put the paper down next to his pipe. "Here, look at this. Joe at work gave me this article from the "Eklund Daily Disappointment" — sorry, the *Daily Post*. He knows I don't take that rag, but there was something he wanted me to see."

"Let me guess. It's about the Indians."

"How'd you know?" He held out the paper for me.

"I don't want to see it. I know what it's about and it's a bunch of crap." The rum was spurring me on.

"Hey, watch your mouth, young lady. Listen to this: "one shack at Thunder Lake was falling apart, with kids running around the yard, stray dogs and cats all over. They lie about their kids to get more welfare and drink up their paychecks—"

"It doesn't say that." I interrupted. "Let me see." I reached over to grab the paper, but he clutched it away from my grasp.

"You didn't wanna see it a minute ago. I'm tellin' ya what's in it. You just can't face the truth about what a sorry, lazy lot the Indians are. They'll never amount to a hill of beans."

I thought of Roland and shot up from my chair; didn't know I could move so fast.

"What the hell's the matter with you?" I hollered without thinking.

Mom came running from the kitchen. "What's going on? What's the ruckus?"

By then, dear old Dad was up, shaking his fist at me. "Don't you cuss at me, you ungrateful bitch." His clenched-fist knuckles turned white.

"Theo," Mom shrieked. "Stop it. You'll have a heart attack."

"Good," I yelled. I bent down for another defiant gulp of rum. "Maybe he'll croak and then … and then …" I knew I'd gone too far.

Dad glared at Mom, his face red, spit flew from his mouth as he roared, "You have an ingrate of a daughter, Clara, who thinks she's too good for us. Your fault … always too soft on her." He took a deep breath and sat down. "Pampering her going to doctors all the time for her back, when she was too damn lazy to stand up straight and have decent posture instead of—"

"Stop it right now," Mom said, a hard edge to her voice I'd never heard. "You get your coat on right now and leave. Go have a drink, I don't care. I want you out of here."

Dad looked at her with wide eyes. "What's with you, Clara? I'm just telling the—"

"Theo, I'm telling you to leave and come back after we're in bed." Mom put her hands to her face. "Thank God that Robin and Peter aren't around. Hope they stay out late."

In shock, I crumpled into the chair. He'd never called me a bitch before. I always figured he wasn't mentally normal, but he really went off the rails tonight. I suppose I did too.

All week he'd served as judge, jury, and executioner for an innocent Indian kid who probably never harmed a fly. I don't know how my old man could be such an ignorant bigot. Mom was just the opposite. How had she put up with him all these years?

Dad seemed to lose steam. His gray hair looked like it was combed with an egg beater; his blue eyes gleamed unnaturally. He stumbled toward the coat closet. "Fine. Fine. I'll go. Always good to get outta here. Be by myself. Drink in peace."

He grumbled as he pulled on his nubby wool coat and gloves. "He turned and scowled at us. "You'll be sorry if I don't come back. Ever." He yanked the front door open, and before stomping out, he growled, "Yup, mark my words, when I'm gone, you'll be singing a different tune."

"Yeah," I mumbled. "Happy Days Are Here Again."

Back in the living room, Mom teared up. "I've never seen him that enraged, talking like that. I'm sorry he took it out on you."

"It's okay, Mom." I circled my arms around her thin shoulders. "I'm used to it."

Years later I would wonder if Mom had been too complacent. She could've stood up for me when Dad mistreated me and not the other two. But maybe it was the times, how she'd been raised. Regardless, at least I had a mother to love.

The question was, what would happen when Theo Borg came back?

CHAPTER 27

Roland
Tuesday . . . Six days later

Rumors intensified. Verbal harassment increased. Nothing physical. Yet.

Students would call out, bolder now. *Hey, Nightbird, trying to crash the party? Got drunk that night, lost your way?* The whole town knew Barbara Gruen did not freeze to death by accident. According to the grapevine, she was strangled or smothered, and Roland Nightbird, Chippewa Indian, had been at the scene after Albert left.

Proof? Not an ounce.

Several days later, Will Sandberg reluctantly had called Roland in. "Look, Roland, we both know how things are. Charlie and I think it may be best if you took a breather and only came in three days a week. And you could leave at three o'clock." He took a drink of coffee and grimaced. "How about taking the day off tomorrow? And you can leave early today before dark for your own safety."

Roland knew he had no choice, although Sandberg's words didn't sound like an order. He'd regret losing his full-time salary, but said, "Okay, I think that's a good idea."

As if reading Roland's mind, Sandberg said, "And I'll talk to someone in finance about compensation. No fair for you to lose money when you're not …" his voice vanished in the air.

"Thanks, Dr. Sandberg, for everything you've done for me."

"Glad I can help. By the way, if anyone wants to question you further, do not talk to them. I'm sure you know this, but there's no evidence to prove any allegations, so you are not obligated to answer more questions from policemen. They shouldn't arrest anyone with insufficient evidence."

Aware of this, Roland had felt relieved to hear Sandberg say it out loud. After thanking the professor again, he'd lumbered out of the office and returned to testing lightbulbs.

●　●　●

At three o'clock, he gathered his things together and slowly left the building. Several students and staff either avoided eye contact or gave Roland the stink eye. Although relieved to escape this place, he still felt he'd been fired for no reason.

Roland drove to Moose's place, knowing he'd need an excuse for arriving early. He knocked, opened the door, and stepped into the living room. A pleasant whiff of woodsmoke and tobacco greeted him. As he tossed his parka onto a chair, Moose sauntered in from his bedroom, stretching and scratching his belly.

"Hey kid." He stifled a yawn. "Whatcha doin' here so early? Boss fire ya?" Moose chuckled.

"Have a seat, Moose. Gotta tell ya something." Exhaustion overtook Roland's mind and body.

"Sounds serious. Lemme get some coffee. You?"

"No thanks." The thought of his uncle's turpentine coffee made him flinch.

Moose brought his cup, and he and Roland settled on the old frayed sofa, its armrests worn to a nub. They stared at an imposing red and black rug hanging on the wall, Moose's one attempt to spruce up the place. His elderly Chippewa friend had woven it years ago, and he refused to put it on the floor. *Too pretty for that. Not gonna have people stomping on it with wet boots.*

Roland finally spoke. "Moose, I hate to tell ya, but you know the investigations about the frozen girl." Moose stiffened and watched him.

"Anyway, long story, but a witness claims he saw me …"

There. It was out. The rest of the story followed.

Moose listened quietly. Then he stood and went toward the kitchen. "Need to doctor up this coffee." This meant he'd splash his moonshine, as he called it, in his cup.

Roland sat with his elbows on his knees, head bent. Moose patted his shoulder as he joined him on the sofa. "This shouldn't be happening to someone like you." He gulped his coffee. "Ahh."

Roland was tempted get plain booze for himself, but waited. "Sorry for all this, Moose. Don't wanna get you or Pa in this mess, but—"

"Guess yer pa don't know yet?" Mapped with wrinkles, Moose's brown face shifted from worry to anger.

"Nah, none of 'em know at home. Hate to tell Pa. You know his temper." Roland winced, recalling his father's drunken rages.

"Well, I'm gettin' mighty pissed off myself right about now." Moose's eyes were slits. "What about yer boss and that professor you like? They doing anything?"

"Not much they can do," Roland sighed. "Just to give me advice and try to keep my spirits up."

Moose scoffed. "Spirits, my ass. What you need is to get the bastards who lied and …"

Roland knew this was going nowhere. Nothing could help. Nothing could be done. Nothing would make a difference. He hated to resign himself to the unfairness of prejudice, but he had no choice. He and his family couldn't fight the system, not to mention centuries of bigotry.

"Moose, I appreciate you taking up for me, but you know there's nothing we can do."

His uncle clanged his cup down on the table. Liquid spilled over the lid onto a crocheted doily. "Damn it. The persecution from the white man will never end. They'll torment us forever."

"Sorry." Roland wanted to end the conversation and rest until supper.

But Moose ranted on. "Oh yeah," he sputtered, "we hear about all the strides we've made, but it never changes. Never!"

He stood, grabbed his cup, and stomped to the kitchen.

Roland saw him dump the coffee in the sink and pour straight booze into the cup. Moose usually didn't get this riled up. Hopefully, he wouldn't drink all night.

When Moose came back to the couch, liquor in hand, Roland said he needed to lie down. Had a headache. Tomorrow he'd go home to his family on the reservation and spend his first day off from work.

Curling up on his cot facing the wall, he pulled the blanket over his head. How would he tell his father the truth about this mess?

CHAPTER 28

Loreen
Wednesday

Pouring her morning orange juice, Loreen looked forward to coffee at Alma's house. She and Will had been walking on eggshells since their verbal clash. All caused by a newspaper article criticizing the Chippewas. She sensed something more preyed on his mind, but she chalked it off to the investigation going nowhere. Or so it seemed. Of course, Will may withhold information to avoid more confrontations.

Loreen leisurely drove north on Birchfront Drive along the lakeshore, taking in the silvery icy crust on Spirit Lake, towering pines, and expensive homes.

Turning onto Alma's driveway, clear of snow, Loreen again admired the Art Deco house, all in white, sweeping curves shaping the structure. A massive bay picture window jutting out like a peninsula showcased a stunning ebony grand piano for all the world to see. Alma had informed her the piano was a Bechstein, owned by her native German father-in-law, who'd shipped it to New York City. Loreen had forgotten how it ended up in Eklund, but somehow it had.

Alma answered the door, dressed as though she were on her way to afternoon tea with the Duchess of Cornwall or some such.

"Darling, come in," she gushed, gently pulling Loreen in the door. "Let me take your coat." Alma helped her friend from her second-best winter coat and hung it in the closet.

Lorene smiled, thanking her. She hadn't worn her best wool coat with the fox wrap. She knew Alma would secretly pity her for trying too hard. Another lesson she'd learned from her mother. *People with real money don't flaunt it.*

They sat in the kitchen, which boasted a splendid view of the lake. "Oh Alma, I never tire of coming to your lovely home."

"Thank you, dear. Always a pleasure to have you." Alma poured them coffee and brought a plate of warm cranberry scones. "A special treat from Georgina. A recipe from her mother." Alma's Scottish housekeeper and cook worked for her three days a week.

Loreen wished she had more friends like Alma. Not to mention a cook.

They chatted about the minutia of everyday life until Alma smoothed her silver hair and leaned forward. "I hear things are heating up on the investigation." She narrowed her eyes at Loreen.

"They certainly are. You've probably heard about that Indian man being a possible suspect in poor Barbara's death. Nightbird his name is. Will knows him, in fact he helped him get that job at the college." Loreen took a breath.

Alma gasped. "Really? I knew Will sympathized with the Chippewas, but … and yes, I'd heard talk about the Indian at duplicate bridge club." Alma lit up a Salem, then softly exhaled a ribbon of smoke. She held the pack of cigarettes toward Loreen, who gladly accepted the offer and soon puffed away with her friend.

"Not only that," Alma continued. "I also ran into Frank Lawson's wife at my cultural arts club, and she said Frank was getting pressure to do something about the allegations, like coerce the cops into arresting Nightbird." Frank, chairman of

Eklund's city council, had added that the situation could become a real debacle.

"You don't say," said Loreen in surprise. "The whole town is in an uproar it seems. But the thing is, there's no hard evidence, so Will says they can't arrest anyone without proof. Although his long Indian scarf that the witness identified is proof to me."

Alma sighed and stamped out her cigarette. "Another Indian in trouble. You remember that column in the *Post* last week. If you ask me, I don't think the government should give them money. They just drink it up."

"I know," Loreen lamented. "What can you do?"

• • •

Later that afternoon, busily slicing chicken into chunks for a hotdish, Loreen heard Will click the front door closed. Stepping away from the counter, she wiped her hands on a towel.

"You're home early," she called. "I've barely started the makings for dinner."

"No hurry." He hung his coat in the closet. "Knox called a meeting this afternoon and sent us home afterward. Said we deserved a break. Our president has a compassionate streak at times." Loreen caught his sarcasm.

"What was the meeting about?" She guessed the answer, but waited for Will.

"The investigation, what else? He's concerned about students and faculty taking sides on accusations against Roland. Hasn't taken a survey. Just his guess."

"I see," Loreen murmured, not wanting another battle on the subject.

Will snatched a Schmidt's from the refrigerator and drank from the bottle. "Things are heating up for the college according to him, and he wants admissions and the deans to downplay the situation. Of course, he's worried about enrollment, but didn't come out and say it."

Will slid into an easy chair and took another swig. "Knox also told us not to say anything to the *Post*. That nosy reporter, Nathan Gill, wanted to interview a few administrators and faculty about the effect of rumors on campus. He already knew that Roland's hours were cut, thanks to my recommendation. Guess word leaked out."

"You don't think that was a good idea?" Loreen blurted. "It would be impossible for the man to keep working with all the harassment." She made her way to the liquor cabinet, poured herself a straight bourbon, and sat in an adjacent chair, forgetting the hotdish for the moment.

"So now you're worried about Roland being harassed? Or you just want him to go away like all the Chippewas?" Will arched his back. His pitch rising. "Then you'll be happy to know the word is spreading from Eklund to other places, like Moorhead and Grand Rapids. Hell, maybe even Duluth. People all over are fascinated with the Indian connection to the murder of a small-town college girl. Nothing happens in winter around here." His words slurred.

"How—" Loreen sputtered.

"Word gets out. And remember the article in the *Post*? The one you agreed with? Well, parts of it made the radio, and word has spread to other newspapers." Will guzzled the rest of his beer and headed for another.

Loreen was fully aware this whole mess had been affecting Will's easygoing personality. And perhaps his mental health?

He returned, gulping from the bottle. "I almost forgot. Tomorrow the *Post* is running an article on the cops now investigating possible suspects, and everyone knows who the prime suspect is."

Loreen perked up. "Really. Is it by the same reporter as—"

"Yes, of course. Nosy Nathan. He'd wormed his way in to interview someone in the mayor's office who informed him there were now suspects. Until now, it was never disclosed in print or on radio, just rumor."

The bourbon nudged Loreen to speak out. "It's about time something is out in the open. People like you just pussyfoot around the Indians as if we haven't done enough for them. Why can't you realize they're different from us?"

"How are they different?" Will's voice was a low roar. "Their skin? Their culture? Their—"

"All of that, you nitwit. Why don't you wake up and smell the coffee? You feel sorry for them … people who do nothing to better themselves—"

"As usual, you don't know what you're talking about," Will shouted. "You don't know the facts. You never went to college. You have no idea about history or statistics or anything. Just your narrow-minded feeble little brain."

He'd never spoken to her like that. Loreen darted up, nearly spilling her drink. "Yeah, I'm just your dumb wife. I was in college once, remember? Then you dragged me up to this godforsaken frozen hell hole with a baby to raise and—"

"As always, your grammar school arithmetic is lacking. You can't even remember when our own son was born—"

"Shut up, you miserable asshole. Just shut up." Loreen took a last drink and slammed the glass onto the end table. Her face felt beet red. "I should've gotten the hell out of here years ago. Except you were nice then. Not anymore. You turned on me, Will. You got cruel." She stomped to the stairs and turned back. "And Loreen Adams was not brought up to be treated like crap. See you around. Don't wait up. Oh yeah, and fix your own damn hotdish."

Loreen pounded up the stairs, and with an animal-like growl, yanked her suitcase from the hall closet.

CHAPTER 29

Roland
Wednesday

Roland awoke to an enticing waft of sizzling bacon, causing his mouth to water. Daylight peeked through the windows. Squinting, he wondered what time it was.

"Hey, sleepy head." Moose wore a plaid flannel shirt and heavy coveralls. "Rise an' shine." His shiny black hair was pulled back in a single braid.

"Did I sleep the whole night through?"

"Indeed you did, son," Moose chuckled. "You were plumb worn out. Come on. Got some bacon and eggs ready for ya." His uncle's sour mood last night had improved. Must've been the booze. A happy hangover.

Roland groaned himself out of bed, washed up, dressed, and sat at the table. "Best bacon and eggs in town, Moose."

"Gotta keep up your strength to tell George about the pickle you're in at the college." Moose slurped his coffee.

"Guess I'll tell him like I told you. Grandma Dinah too." Roland wiped his mouth. "Maybe I'll luck out and nobody else will be around."

"You'll do good, kid. I'll put in a good word to my ancestor, the medicine man. He'll protect ya."

Roland doubted Moose really believed that, but he didn't ask.

•   •   •

When Roland arrived at the reservation, everything looked the same as always. Nothing ever changed. He drove into his make-do driveway, noticing patches of dirt among the dog-pee yellowed snow.

"I'm here," Roland called, opening the door. "Got my grip. Staying the night."

"Well, get in here, boy." Dinah ambled toward him. "Let me take your bag."

"How do, Nani." She was a breath of fresh air to Roland. Her long braids looked grayer than they had two weeks ago, but her wise black eyes sparkled like ebony.

He tossed his bag on the bed and returned to the sitting room, flopping down on the battered couch. He took the orange juice Dinah offered him.

"Hungry?" Always her first question to anyone who walked in.

"Thanks, but I just had Moose's bacon and eggs."

"Mine are better," Dinah snorted.

The door opened, and George called out. "Hey, what's my favorite son doing here? Last I checked, it ain't the weekend."

"Well now, I don't rightly know," Dinah said, probably perturbed at herself for not noticing.

"Hey, Pa." Roland set his juice on the table. "Better sit down when you get settled."

"Hm. Sounds serious." George sat on the sofa by Roland, a frown etched on his dark, granite face.

Roland gave a quick cough. "Um, you know about the frozen girl at the college—"

"What about it?" Patience was not George's strong point.

"Okay, but don't fly off the handle." Roland repeated the same story he'd told Moose yesterday. George stared ahead; jaw clenched. It seemed like an hour before Roland finished speaking.

George and Dinah had listened to the whole tale in silence. Not a good sign.

"Oh, Jesus, Mary, and Joseph," Dinah moaned. "How can they do that? Getting you to cut your hours. You did nothing. Why are they—"

"You know damn well why," George burst out. He bolted from the couch and paced back and forth, panting loudly.

"It'll be all right in the long run," said Roland, trying to appease his father. "The rumors about me will die down. Nothing to get in an uproar—"

"Don't tell me what to do, boy. I'll get pissed if I want to. Good reason for it."

"Simmer down, George. You'll have a heart attack." Dinah wiped her forehead.

"Goddammit, they're doing it again. Always—"

"Who?" Dinah asked.

"The white man. Who else?" George's voice at a slightly lower pitch.

He ranted on, his words and anger echoing Moose's and no doubt the universal anger of generations of Indians.

"And damn near firing you," George snarled. "I'm gonna report this to the tribal council. See if they can do anything—"

"Oh, heaven on earth, what can they do? Have an uprising?" sighed Dinah.

Roland hoped Dinah was kidding. And he hoped pa was just blowing hot air.

"Can you stay for early supper?" Dinah changed the subject.

"Sorry, Nani, but I need to get back to Moose's." Roland stood and straightened his washed-out jeans. "Promised to help him fix a couple boards on the bait shop."

"Harumph," George spouted. "Go ahead then. But I'll be calling Moose to see what's happening. Mark my words, I'm going to the council. Those bastards can't get away with—"

"All right, George." Dinah hoisted herself out of her chair. "Roland, do you remember when I first taught you the legend of the Wendigo monster?"

"How could I forget?" He was chomping at the bit to get out of there.

"I'll pray to the Spirit for the horrible beast to descend on Eklund and—"

"Now, Ma. Folks these days don't believe—"

"You don't know for sure, son. My great grandfather told me—"

"Nani, sorry, but I have to go." With that, Roland escaped to his old jalopy, fired it up, and hit the road.

Driving back to Moose's, he thought more about that fateful night at the crime scene.

He reminded himself that only Jasper knew the truth. At least nobody claimed to have seen Jasper.

Roland would never tell a soul the real truth. Not even close family or Sandberg or anyone. Of course, Albert was there and could also lie and say he'd seen Roland. But then he'd be placing himself at the scene. Partygoers said he was flirting with Barbara and a few said they saw him leave after her. So, how could he claim to have seen Roland without implicating himself? And right now, no hard evidence existed that anyone was near Barbara's body. Just the witness's statement. But the rumors had spread like wildfire that Albert and Roland were there. Naturally, both had denied it.

But he finally convinced himself that neither he nor Albert would spill the beans about one another's presence that night. Each one had too much to lose. They'd both shoot themselves in the foot.

One thing he knew for sure. As Roland's grandfather used to say, they were between the hammer and the anvil.

CHAPTER 30

Nancy
Friday

Was that sun filtering its way through my curtains? What a shock to wake up to light rather than gloom. As I went through the morning ritual of preparing for the day, it occurred to me that Barbara had passed away four weeks ago. I couldn't decide if time had flown or crept at a snail's pace.

I smoothed my bed and thought of the diary. Maybe soon.

• • •

Eager for the weekend, I nearly sprinted out of my poetry class. Thank God I could relax for a couple days. How could I stand it until student teaching began in April, and I could ditch this place? My friend Gail and I had made arrangements to rent an apartment in Green Earth, a small town 35 miles from Eklund.

In the hallway, I spotted Roland slinking toward me, hugging the wall. His eyes were glued to the floor, but I wanted to say hi to the poor guy.

"Morning, Roland. I missed seeing you yesterday."

Roland looked up, startled. "How do, Nancy." Clearly uncomfortable, he eyeballed the other students sauntering here and there.

I hesitated. "Were you here yesterday?"

"Ah, guess folks will notice anyway. Dr. Sandberg and Charlie thought it best if I cut my hours and just work three times a week." He scuffed his bear-sized feet. "You know, the rumors worse and —"

"For God's sake. So, it's come to that. That really pisses me off." I was at a loss for words. "I'm so … so damn sorry, pardon my French."

Roland sighed. "Thanks, Nancy. Your French is the least of my worries."

I laughed in spite of myself. "You still have a sense of humor in all this. But really, what a shame you have to put up with this crap. So unfair." The small gap between his front teeth gave him an endearing, innocent look.

"Yeah, well, you learn to live with it. Out of my hands." Roland turned. "I better get going. I … I really appreciate your…" His words tapered away.

"Hey, it's all right. Like I said, lots of us are on your side." I watched him trudge away, his head bent. Once again, I thought of most people not bothering to accuse that asshole Albert of anything. Why would they? When the Indian guy can be their scapegoat.

The sun still hovered in the sky as I strolled home. What a relief to detect a slight hint of spring in the air. More snow had melted into slush puddles, cropping up on lawns and curbs. I didn't worry about slipping and falling as much. But I didn't get my hopes up for an Indian summer yet. Snow would most likely return to torment us.

•   •   •

I relaxed at home for a couple hours before my dear father graced us with his presence by banging in the front door. Our home had become thick with tension since he'd stormed out a couple weeks ago following our knock-down-drag-out. After Mom kicked him out, he'd returned later that night long after I fell asleep. We've walked on thin ice ever since.

He grunted a hello to my sister Robin and me sitting on the sofa. "Almost time for the news." His gold watch was tucked in his pocket, but the chain dangled down in a straight line; not clipped to his vest. He'd probably had a snort at work.

"Lucky us," I spoke in a low voice to Robin. "Wonder what it would be like to watch the news without him around."

"You'll find out soon enough when you're living in Green Earth, lucky bum." Robin reached for a potato chip. "Then me and Peter will be stuck here on our own."

"And poor Mom. Maybe when we all fly the coop she'll take off too." I knew that was highly doubtful.

My father returned, drink in hand, and settled into the easy chair. "Got the right channel, Robin?" He didn't speak to me these days.

"Yup." Robin crunched another chip.

After Douglas Edwards announced a plane explosion over Hawaii killing everyone on board, the broadcast faded into Speedy's irritating jingle, "plop-plop, fizz-fizz, oh what a relief it is!" It would be a relief all right, if my father would keep still. But that wish proved short-lived.

"Say, Robin. Maybe you've heard the rumors about the frozen girl. Saw the paper at work. That reporter said there's a suspect now. First time in print."

Knowing better, I blurted, "God, at least get the facts right, like you never do. Nosy Nathan Gill, eminent journalist, wrote about *some* suspects the police are looking at."

I knew why the old geezer zeroed in on that. He could kill two birds with one stone: blame the Indian and get my goat.

"Aw, smart-assed as ever, are ya." He drained his glass. "For your information, it's all over town that Indian Joe did something to that girl. He was right there at the scene."

Without warning, my pressure cooker burst. I shot from the couch and without a thought, threw my glass of gin and ice at him, missing my target. It landed on the carpet by his feet, spilling the contents and cracking the glass. Good thing Mom was in the basement doing laundry.

His jaw dropped to the floor. "Why you scrawny witch." He stood up, wobbly. "Now look what you've done."

I lost my train of thought and gazed at the broken glass. "What do I care? Except Mom will have to clean it up."

He also gaped at the shards of glass, dumbfounded.

"Bad enough you're such a narrow-minded bastard, but to poison Robin and Peter with your opinions and lies, lies, lies."

His face turned blood-red. "You're a lousy excuse for a daughter. You can just go to your pal … yeah, you're probably friends with Injun' Joe. Too bad he's not white. Then you might finally have a boyfriend." He growled, stamping to the kitchen for another Jim Beam.

I clenched my teeth and fists. I should be afraid of him, but instead I wished for a fresh glass to throw at him.

Robin came beside me and lowered her voice. "Just try and ignore the SOB. You know how he gets."

I panted, my shoulders rising and falling, a boxer ready to fight. "Yeah, but the thing is … the worst thing is he'll influence you and Peter with his bias—"

"No, he won't. Me and Peter are old enough to think for ourselves. We both know Indian kids. We know what Dad says is a bunch of bullshit."

I patted her shoulder. "I still worry."

Then it dawned on me, once and for all, that I could not … would not live under his roof any longer. I couldn't last until student teaching. I had to go now. Go where? I'd figure something out.

I took several deep breaths and strode into the kitchen where both parents putzed around, Mom with a basket of unfolded clothes.

"I'm not living here anymore," I announced. "I refuse to live under his roof. So, in a few days, I'm gone."

Dad tossed his head and started for the living room. "Good riddance," he muttered.

Mom's eyes pooled with tears. "Oh, Nancy, you don't mean that. It's only a few weeks until —"

"I'm sorry, Mom. I can't stand it that long. I hate to leave you, but he's killing me. If I can't concentrate on school, I'm done for." I knew I was stretching things, but I really couldn't hack it anymore.

"But … but where will you go? Do you know yet?" Her wrinkles looked like a map.

"I've made arrangements," I lied.

"Where then? We don't have relatives around that you could stay with. Must be Judy or Peggy?"

"Yeah, them," I stammered. I hugged Mom. Her bones seemed to protrude into my hands. "Don't worry. I'll come home off and on to get different clothes and stuff. When he's at work."

"All right. I feel a little better." Her soft brown eyes studied me. "I'll still miss you."

I know, Mom. I'll always love you."

I patted her shoulder and headed downstairs before I fell apart.

Tomorrow I'd approach Peggy about sleeping on her sofa bed in her living room. It would be a tight fit in her one-bedroom apartment, but it could work. If not, I'd ask Judy as a last resort if she could let me use a guest room, but I doubted Loreen would agree. She griped about putting up the Gruens for a few days. I can imagine her reaction if Judy asked if I could stay.

I sure put myself between a rock and a hard place.

CHAPTER 31

Loreen
Saturday

Loreen awoke at the crack of dawn in a bed that felt like a washboard. God, how she missed her own bedroom. She stretched, her thoughts slipping back to several days ago when she checked into the White Birch Motel. How ironic. The same place she'd stashed the Gruens after they'd arrived for Barbara. Good Lord, four weeks ago today? Yes, four weeks since her life turned upside down.

Last Wednesday, after that god-awful fight with Will, she'd thrown some random clothes in her suitcase and snapped it shut. Before anyone knew, she'd slammed the front door and made a beeline for the garage. Since she wasn't serious about heading for her parents' home in Chicago, she'd registered at the motel. Although anger still coursed through her veins, she felt a sense of freedom. After all, she was momentarily an independent woman.

Today, Loreen planned breakfast at Clyde's Café, and a stop at the library to browse and read. The last two days she'd popped home when Will was working. At first, Judy was aghast at the sight of her mother. *Mom, you're here! Where did you go last night? I was worried sick! We figured you'd probably be safe, but you should've called.*

Loreen had reassured her she was only a few blocks away at the White Birch, and she'd probably come home in a week or so. That is, if she and Will could work through this personal adversity.

Still in her nightgown on the rock-hard bed, she jumped when the telephone buzzed. She groped for the receiver and picked up. "Hello? Oh, hi, Judy. How are—"

"Listen, Mom. Rumors at the college are escalating." Loreen knew what her daughter meant. "The talk is getting worse about Roland being at the scene, you know—"

"Yes, I know. Go on. What else?" Loreen felt like a bloodhound.

"Dad and Charlie cut back his hours, so he's only working two or three days a week. Nancy feels sorry for him, but I'm not sure anymore." Judy took a breath. "Then Albert's dad came from Crookston and went to the cops, you know the main ones working on the case."

"Really." Loreen sat up, more curious than ever.

"He wanted them to drop Albert as a suspect because the only witness was totally unreliable, couldn't see Al's face in the storm, blah, blah. And then the dad says he was sure the other guy's scarf was Roland's."

"Well, he has a point." Loreen fished a cigarette out of her purse and lit up.

Judy continued. "Then the dad told them that the Indian was the only obvious suspect, and Bergstrom, the cop, should be aiming for him and leave Albert alone. He'd asked why would his son harm someone like Barbara?"

Loreen exhaled, filling the room with a haze of smoke. "Didn't I hear she may have rejected him?"

"Oh, Mother. That's what the kids are saying, but the more I think about it, I'm not sure I see Al doing that. Even though he's a first-class asshole."

"How do you know all this, hon?"

"Bergstrom came to Dad's office the next day and told him the whole story. How Mr. Melowski was like his son, an arrogant bully who thought he had a right to march in the police station barking orders."

"You know, dear, parents will defend their children to the end. I certainly would." Loreen brushed an ash off the sleeve of her nightgown.

"I know, Mom. I gotta go." A pause. "I guess I won't see you here at the house since Dad's home. Maybe I'll stop by the motel tomorrow. I'll call ya. Bye." Judy hung up, and Loreen visualized her hurrying off somewhere important, her auburn pony tail swinging in the breeze.

As she showered and dressed for her big day at Clyde's and the library, Loreen couldn't decide whether she'd call Alma to exchange the latest gossip on the investigation. She'd been too embarrassed to tell her friend about leaving Will and staying in this drab little room.

The thing was, Alma had a solid fifty-year marriage before Harry's heart attack, so she may not take kindly to Loreen running out on an esteemed professor like Will. She'd better keep her situation under wraps.

After all, only common women stay in motels. Not someone like Loreen Sandberg.

CHAPTER 32

Nancy
Saturday

I woke up with a sense of dread. Today, I needed to follow through on my threat to leave, figure out another place to stay. Hard to grasp that yesterday's outburst might materialize.

An hour later, I tiptoed up the basement stairs to the kitchen, listening for signs of my revered father. Sometimes he'd go to the station on weekends. Had to check if the trains were running on time without his divine guidance.

I cracked the door open and peeked in. Mom stood by the stove in her wash-worn chenille housecoat, flipping bacon in the black skillet.

"Psst. Mom, is he around?"

She turned toward me. "Oh, hello, dear," she whispered. "He's in the living room, but he's leaving in a few minutes. Come on. Have some breakfast." Her skin hung like melted wax. Had I caused my mother to age overnight?

She grabbed a plate for me and was about to put a slab of bacon on it. "No thanks, Mom. I'll just have juice and coffee."

"You need more than that to keep up your strength. At least eat some toast and cereal."

Maybe I could force down a piece of toast. "Okay. Can't have you worrying any more than you already are."

As I dropped a slice of bread into the toaster, my father called, "Clara. I'm leaving now."

His voice growing louder, he stepped into the kitchen. "I'll be back … what the hell are you doing here?"

"I still live here, you know." I nonchalantly plucked the toast from the toaster. "Not for long, but—"

"Won't be soon enough." He snorted and went off in a huff.

"Sorry, Mom. I can't eat this. I'll sit and have coffee with you before I go."

While we lamented the state of our lives, Robin and Peter, scruffy from sleep, stumbled in.

"I see Dad didn't kill you before he left." Peter flung the refrigerator door open.

"You should be a detective," I said. "I'll be around to irritate you for a few days yet."

Robin sat down by me. "I wish you weren't going, Nance." She stared at my coffee cup.

"Jeez, Robin, you and Mom look like a couple of sad sacks. I'm not moving to Siberia. I'll be back every few days to get in your hair." I couldn't afford to get all blubbery. There were plans to make. And soon.

● ● ●

Later at Peggy's apartment, she offered me glazed doughnuts and the usual Saturday coffee.

"Thanks, Peg. I sure needed this. Um, delicious." I chewed slowly, relishing the sweet vanilla taste, soft and gooey.

"You look frazzled," she said.

"Yup, more than usual. All this business about Roland is getting me down." We lit up cigarettes. I'd quit later. Famous last words.

We commiserated about the investigation for a few minutes with nothing new to add. All useless chatter. We longed for answers. Who caused Barbara's death?

"I do have something to ask you, Peg." I took a sip of the tepid coffee. "You know how my dad's been getting worse about his prejudices and the fights we've had?"

"Yeah, he's always been a pain in the ass to live with. Not as bad as my old man, but still ..." Peggy got the peculator and poured us fresh coffee. "I hoped things would improve when your mom kicked him out for the night."

"Right, but he didn't. Couldn't keep still last night ... worse than ever. Trying to browbeat Robin and Peter into believing his crap about Roland. Then he turns on me, and I blew my stack like never before."

"Good heavens." Peggy reached for a doughnut.

"So, everything went to hell, and I ended up yelling I was gonna leave. Live somewhere else until I go student teaching. You remember I signed for a place in Green Earth with Gail Bell?"

Peggy nodded. "Didn't her mom have polio and uses crutches?"

"Yes, really sad." I put out my cig.

"Reminds me of seeing the rows and rows of iron lungs in the movie news reels."

"I remember that too. I wondered how the patients could stand lying there, like trapped in a submarine or something." My mind snapped back to the here and now.

"So anyway, I'm afraid to ask, but is there some way I could sleep on your sofa bed for a couple weeks? I wouldn't clutter up the place. I'd go home when he's at work and do laundry and stuff."

"Gee, Nance, I wanna help out, but this place is so small. What about Judy? They have two guestrooms."

"I know, but I figured Loreen would have a hissy fit if Judy asked her. Can you picture it? She barely let the Gruens stay for a couple days." I scoffed. "Besides, she looks down her nose at me."

"Join the club. I gotta agree you're probably right not staying there."

"And like Mom said, we don't have relatives in town, so I have to beg, which I hate."

"It's fine. Lord, we've been friends practically all our lives. Pack your bags and come on in. We'll make due. We'll have our own slumber party."

Somehow, the thought didn't appeal to me like it did when we were kids. Judging from Peggy's thin smile, she felt the same way.

CHAPTER 33

Roland
Monday

Roland was barely inside Moose's door after finishing work. "Yer pa wants you to call him," Moose said.

"Hm. Okay, but I may not wanna hear what he has to say." He flung his coat and knapsack on the chair.

"Dunno about that. I'll hold my tongue till he's done talkin'." Moose lit a cigar, sucking in several times, his lips puckered like he was savoring a pickle.

"I'll call now. Get it over with." Roland picked up the receiver and told the operator his dad's number. Maybe he'd luck out and the line would be busy.

"Hello," George groused.

"Heard you called, Pa." Roland leaned forward in the chair.

"Son, I'll get right to the point. Want you to know that yesterday I met with some men on the council. Told 'em about how you're in hot water for something you didn't do. Told the whole story, and they swere all up in arms about the rumors and you getting your hours sliced."

"Oh God," Roland said. "What did you do? I hope it doesn't go any farther—"

"It just might. There was talk they'd march into Eklund and boycott businesses."

"Boycott? What places? Why would that—"

"Listen," George interrupted. "As you know, some of us do banking in Eklund, plus shop the tool stores and garden nurseries. Plus stores like the Five and Dime. We do more business in town than just go to the courthouse and liquor stores like people think."

"But how would that make a difference? The town wouldn't care. Indians don't spend that much."

"You'd be surprised, mister. Store owners could see a dip in their—"

Roland moaned. "The college folk would hate me more than they do now." He looked at Moose, shaking his head in frustration.

Moose shrugged and snuffed out his cigar and didn't speak.

"I still don't think—"

"Yeah, yeah," George said. "One last thing. Dinah's sister was snubbed by a clerk at Ben Franklin last week; the woman took a month of Sundays to wait on her. That tells ya how bad things are."

Roland said his goodbyes and hung up. He didn't know Moose's opinion, but he was sick and tired of talking. The conversation would've gone on forever.

•   •   •

Polishing off the last of his supper of fried egg and bacon sandwiches, Roland stifled a yawn. A nap sure sounded good. Moose, scarfing down his third sandwich, sopped up runny yellow yoke with soggy toast. Unappetizing sight, but a hearty meal.

"Ya know, kid, I've wondered a few times where you were the whole time you walked to the college that night the frozen girl..." Moose's words stuck in the air.

Buying time, Roland pretended not to hear. "What?"

Moose repeated the question.

"Like I said before, I got lost in the blizzard. I kinda led Jasper 'cause I know the sidewalks and streets better, but he lagged behind a lot."

"Yeah, but if you'd walked all that time, you—"

"We were freezing and couldn't see squat, took wrong turns, ended up going opposite ways sometimes." I'd explained this to Moose before. "All a mess. And my memory is ... I don't remember a lot. Just one big freezing blur."

Roland hoped Moose would be satisfied and not ask again. But was he suspicious?

"Okay." Moose slurped the rest of his coffee and started clearing the table. "I can see everything muddled together in your mind. One time, me and some pals tried to drive home from someone's shack, and the snow was blowin' like a house a' fire, and ..."

Roland tuned out the words of Moose's time-worn story. Finally, after the dishes soaked in the sink, Roland lay down on his cot.

• • •

He must've dozed off for at least a couple hours when the phone jarred Roland awake.

"Hello," Moose answered. "What, George?" Moose paused, listening. "Really? You don't say. Well, I'll be a monkey's uncle."

Why was pa calling again? Roland bolted beside his uncle. Moose said, "Just a sec, George. Here's your boy."

"Pa?" Roland gripped the clunky black receiver. "What's going on?"

"You should hear this, kid." George sounded weary. "A few council men are going into Eklund tomorrow morning to see the mayor and the cops. They'll threaten a boycott if the cops don't back off thinkin' you're a suspect. They'll demand that you be dropped off the suspect list."

Roland groaned under his breath. He wondered how the tribal council would be able to speak to the mayor and the cops. Especially the mayor. Don't you need clout to speak to him?

George continued. "Hate to tell you this son, cuz you won't like it. They might go to the college too and talk to the president."

"Whaat?" Roland yelped. "No. No. They can't do that. It'll make things worse for me. What are they gonna say? That Knox should announce to the students they need to be nice to the Indian? He might be innocent!" God, this was a nightmare.

"Simmer down, son. They probably won't make it that far. Not tomorrow anyway."

Roland kept moaning. Beads of sweat dripped in his eyes. "They gotta be organized. Who's gonna lead the group? They can't all talk at once."

"Jake and Red Horse. Jake will do most of the talking," George said. "He's negotiated with the white man for years."

Everyone on Thunder Lake knew that Jake Waters and Red Horse Jones were the unofficial spokesmen for the tribe. Both were weathered, intelligent Chippewas whose families had been around for generations. If you had troubles, you went to them for help. That is, if you were a law-abiding resident yourself.

Roland handed the phone to Moose without saying goodbye to his father. He didn't trust himself to keep a civil tongue. A grinding rage made him want to lash out and beat somebody.

Plodding to his cot, he took three deep breaths. His life was getting worse by the hour. What could he do?

Roland listened to Moose mumbling for several more minutes before saying good night to George.

Moose must've sensed this wasn't the time for further talking, so he poured himself a beer and settled in with last year's copy of *The Farmer's Weekly*.

Roland pictured Jake and Red Horse walking down the college halls, drawing stares and comments, before barging into President Knox's office

There had to be an answer. A solution. Something he could do. But what?

CHAPTER 34

Nancy
Tuesday

I borrowed Peggy's rundown Plymouth this afternoon when I knew my father would be at work. I was already packed, so Mom and I lugged some clothes and a suitcase up the basement stairs and out to the car. I hoped eagle-eyed Mrs. Larson across the street wasn't peeking out her curtains to spy on me. The neighbors knew I'd be leaving next month, but not before.

"Don't worry about her." Mom flung a bag of linen in the trunk. "Who cares what she thinks."

"I know, but she'll just hound you until you tell her the truth about my fight with Dad."

Otherwise, I didn't give a damn what the old biddy or any other neighbors thought.

After twenty minutes, I hugged Mom goodbye. "I'll see you in a couple days."

"Nancy dear, I wish …" she wiped away a tear.

"I'll be right around the corner, you know. Call me anytime."

As I drove off, guilt weighed me down like a leaden yoke.

• • •

I opened the car trunk and took two light-weight bags to haul upstairs to Peggy's apartment. She'd given me a key, so I made two more trips and the job was done. With my back condition, climbing up and down stairs was killing my spine, but I'd pop some aspirin. Wish I had a few of Peggy's Miltown.

After sipping a Coke on the couch, I unpacked my stuff in an empty dresser drawer and closet Peggy had arranged. The sofa bed would be awkward, but we'd fold it up during the day, leaving the sheets on. A guestroom would be nice, but beggars can't complain. Not out loud, anyway.

Later, when Peggy and I finished our dinner of Swanson chicken pot pies and raspberry sherbets for dessert, we took coffee into the living room and lounged on the sofa.

Peg lit a Winston and exhaled. "I saved some big news for now."

"What? What happened?"

"Word got around the office that the Thunder Lake tribal council marched into town this morning to complain about Roland's situation."

"I can't believe it," I gasped. "Never heard of that before."

"I think it's happened in the past, and my boss said there were about six men in the group. Two older ones did the talking."

For once I kept quiet to let Peg go on.

She tucked her yellow hair behind her ears. "Somehow, they finagled their way in and talked to Mayor Rice himself, along with some others. The Indian leaders said they put up with enough bias from the town, but to accuse Roland and not the white kid was beyond unfair. Something must be done about it, or the tribe would boycott businesses, withdraw their money from banks, and other things."

Crushing out her cigarette, she went on. "Then they marched up the street to the cop station and demanded to talk to the police chief. I think his name's Bill McIntire. Anyway, unlucky for him, he was in his office, so they informed him the cops should take Roland off the suspect list and announce he's innocent. Or the mayor will be on their back about the boycott threat."

"Good God," I exclaimed. "What next?"

"You tell me. The whole thing is getting ridiculous. Anyway, their squabbling went on and on. Don't know what the cops said. Probably tried to smooth it over."

"Jeez. Unbelievable." I stood holding my cup. "Can I spice up my coffee? Do you still have the amaretto I got you for Christmas?"

"Of course. I didn't drink the whole bottle. That stuff's strong."

I poured us each more coffee and splashed a little liqueur in our cups. "Maybe this'll help stimulate the reading I have to do tonight for my Hawthorne class."

I sank into the sofa. "Umm, great coffee. Well, that was big news today. It's—"

"There's more," Peggy said. "After the cops, they marched over to the college!"

My jaw dropped. "No! Why?"

"They were determined to find President Knox and demand he does something about the kids harassing Roland. They said they realize people's opinions can't be controlled, but the administration can help prohibit verbal comments directed at Roland. I guess that's what they said."

I shook my head. "I agree with what the Indians are trying to do for Roland, but how can anyone monitor that? If kids say smartass remarks to Roland, what's going to happen? No one's going to report anyone, and if they did, what would the punishment be?"

"I know," Peggy agreed. "The tribe's living in a dream world."

"God, what a mess." I took a healthy swig of my doctored-up coffee. Exhaustion overcame me. "I really gotta hit the books. I can read in the kitchen or—"

"No, let's make up the sofa bed. Stretch out and be comfy. I have a new Photoplay mag, so that'll keep me busy. I'd rather read Hawthorne, but I know you won't let me, ha ha."

"Right. Rub it in. Seriously, thanks again for letting me stay, Peg. You're a—"

"You don't need to keep thanking me. I'll give you the rental bill when you leave."

• • •

After trying to absorb the allegory in *The Marble Faun*, I gave up and readied myself for bed. I said my goodnights to Peggy and I turned out the lights. What an exhausting day.

Weary as I was, sleep eluded me. Images of Indians and Roland kept nagging my mind. How could the tribal demands ever be realized? It seemed a solution for this whole dilemma was out of reach.

CHAPTER 35

Loreen
Tuesday

For the past three days, Loreen had been more anxious than ever. Will had agreed to work on a reconciliation. Their marriage was at stake, which scared the hell out of her. Maybe she could fake more sympathy toward the Indians just to keep peace. So far, their marriage was basically a nonaggression pact, not ideal, but better than living in that gloomy motel.

Loreen rumpled Soldier's furry neck, and he licked her hand with his salmon tongue. "I'd miss you, buddy. I'll try not to move anywhere."

Popping another Seconal, she heard Will at the front door. She thrust the sleeping pills back in their hiding place behind her estrogen tablets. Will would object to sleeping pills. Estrogen? Fine with that. She shut the medicine cabinet, gave her reflection a confident glance, and hurried downstairs.

"How was your day, Will? I hope—"

"It's been a god-awful day." He hung his coat and hat in the closet "We both need to sit down with a strong drink." He went to the liquor cabinet and prepared two stiff whiskey highballs.

"Oh God. I'm afraid to hear." If things had escalated with the Indians, Loreen would stay calm and watch her words. The pill and drink should relax her.

Once seated, Will lifted his highball and swallowed deeply. "May as well get right to it. Just try hard not to get upset. This morning, tribal representatives from Thunder Lake marched into town. Long story, but they were able to speak to Knox and …" Will continued to relay the rest of the saga.

Loreen listened intently to the entire story without uttering a word. She felt a bubbling deep in her stomach. And then the heat. It permeated her entire body like a hot flash. The sheer audacity of Indians making demands from people like her.

"I'm holding it in, Will. I'm trying my damndest to hold it in." Her voice, eerily low and even, heat rising to her throat.

"Take two deep breaths. Then a sip of booze." Will leaned toward his wife. "I can see you're making an effort."

"Making an effort, Will? Making an effort?" Lorene's voice still chillingly steady. "Yes, I, Professor Sandberg's wife of twenty-five years, must make an effort." She was burning up, losing her senses.

Will patted her arm. "Everything will be all right." Was that fear showing in his face? "Let me refresh your drink."

It happened. The volcano erupted with venomous rage.

"This is it! I can't keep quiet!" Loreen rose in a fury. Her drink splashed over as she bumped the coffee table with her leg. "The Indians are ruining everything … our lives, our town … everything." She stood next to Will, her arms dancing in the air.

"What was this charade of theirs, making demands like they have a right?" she sputtered. "Like Sitting Bull or whatever? They've been circling the wagons ever since this Rol … Reuben … whatever the hell his name is was seen there that night."

Will stood. He tried to reach her arm, but she jerked away. "Loreen, you have to be calm. Now sit down and pull yourself together."

"Ha! The only thing I'll pull together is your balls. That is if you ever get any." Her screaming lowered a few decibels. "You've never understood, and you never will. Haven't the whites given them enough? Welfare money so they can breed more kids, drink, and never pull themselves up by the bootstraps like our ancestors did. They're an inferior race, Will. Shouldn't mingle with us. They're just a drain on our country, just like the—"

"Go! Now!" Will bellowed. "Get out of my sight. I won't have you poisoning our children with your ... your Nazi beliefs."

"Oh, for God's sake, wake up. Judy's too old anymore to ... and Rod's not even—"

"I said, go!" Will shouted again. He took her arm and pushed her toward the stairs.

"Let go of me, you bastard!" Loreen wrestled him off her, but he grabbed her again. She balled up her fists and tried to belt him in the jaw, but missed. Instead, grazed his neck.

Will stiffened. "Good Lord, what are we doing?"

"I'll tell you what I'm doing. I'm going home where I've belonged all these years. Too bad you changed, Will. We would've had a chance. But now ..." Loreen raced up the stairs, half muttering, half sobbing.

"I haven't changed," Will called after her. "You've turned into someone I don't know. A ... a toxic stranger."

"I'm not speaking to you anymore, so you can just stay mad." Loreen yelled from the top stair.

Will drooped down in his chair. "My anger won't last. But my sorrow might."

• • •

By noon the next day, Loreen Sandberg was on her way home.

CHAPTER 36

Roland
Wednesday

On Tuesday when the Chippewas had trooped into Eklund, they'd caused quite a commotion with city officials and townspeople alike, according to the radio. No surprise to Roland. He knew the event would be a firestorm sure to burn him.

Today, when Moose dropped him off for work, Roland dreaded the gauntlet from the car to his cubicle in Main Hall. He slowly emerged from the front seat. "Guess I can't wait forever, Moose. See ya later."

"You'll be fine, kid. Just hold your head up. Show 'em you have pride." In spite of his upbeat words, Moose's cheeks sagged with weariness and resignation.

Roland waved. "Thanks." Regret and guilt clung to him. Why did his uncle have to get mixed up in this? All he does is worry.

He no sooner opened the main door, and it started.

"Hey, Nightbird, ya gonna have an uprising?" Someone called out.

Others joined in as Roland lowered his head, ignoring the hecklers.

"Yer relatives got their tomahawks ready?"

"Hear they wanna take over the town now."

"How many scalps you gonna get on your belt after ya—"

Just as the thugs slowly began to surround Roland, a voice roared, "Hey!" The creeps stiffened in their tracks.

"Shut up right now, or you're all going on report." The voice belonged to Mr. Walton, a big, burly dean from the administration office. He grabbed two of the jerks by their shirt cuffs.

"Do you want to come with me or shut your traps?" Walton probably outweighed both the creeps put together.

The guys didn't seem so tough now. They mumbled undecipherable words to the dean, and he let them go. He leered at the gathered group as though mentally making note of faces.

"That goes for the rest of you or anybody who verbally harasses, taunts, or bullies anyone on this campus."

He shook his head in disgust. "This isn't romper room, people. You're in college, for God's sake. What are your parents gonna think when they get a letter from me? Now get out of my sight and go to class." Walton wiped his brow.

Roland slouched awkwardly against a pillar, hopefully hidden from view. The students slithered away, and Walton caught Roland's eye and walked over. "Damn it, Roland, I can't tell you how sorry I am. Bunch of assholes. Between you and me, I'd kick them out if I could."

Roland scuffled his feet, head downward. "Yeah, well I … just don't know. I—"

"I can imagine." Walton patted his shoulder. "For now, just carry on. Hold your chin up, and keep reminding yourself that this won't last. There's always a turn in the road ahead."

"Thanks, Mr. Walton." Roland knew the dean as a nice guy who cared about him, like Dr. Sandberg. But his chewing out the kids taunting him was beyond embarrassing. He had never felt so humiliated in his life.

Roland wondered if Walton had ever experienced that feeling.

• • •

Again, in his workplace, Roland stayed sequestered in his own general area, secluded from more student goading. Of course, he couldn't stay isolated forever. Sometime he'd be needed in other parts of campus. However, he appreciated Charlie's assigning him work close by.

After lunch, he tossed his paper bag in the trash and continued sorting inventory forms.

He heard footsteps and looked up.

"Hello, Roland," Will Sandberg said. "Pretty quiet around here."

Roland looked up. "Yeah, it's been okay." He didn't mention the Walton scene.

"Sorry to interrupt your work, but could you step in for a minute?" Sandberg's voice weary.

"Yes, sir." A pit formed in his belly. Sandberg never had good news these days.

Seated stiffly in his usual chair, Roland waited for Sandberg's words.

"You probably kept a low profile yesterday when the tribal spokesmen came to town." Sandberg waited, but Roland didn't respond. "You're aware they visited the mayor, police, and President Knox?"

"Yes, sir. Heard it from my dad and the radio last night."

"Roland, I won't waste time telling you how sorry I am. You know that. I want you to understand the conversation with Dr. Knox. First of all, Red Horse Jones demanded the college should ban all verbal intimidation of you and of Indians in general. As punishment, offenders would be suspended for one or two days."

Roland scoffed. "That's really unrealistic, it should've been obvious to the council." Roland hadn't heard those details.

"Yes," Sandberg agreed. "Impossible to enforce. Who would report their friends to the dean? Students don't know the names of everyone. The whole idea is preposterous."

"A real joke, but not funny," Roland said. "What did Dr. Knox say?"

"At first, he said they'd see what solution they could come up with. He tried to smooth it out as best he could and shooed them out as gently as possible."

"All this because of me." Roland's cheeks sagged.

"We talked last night with several faculty members, and they will issue a campus-wide memo for all instructors to read in class. The message will state the danger of bias in a society and then focus on Eklund and its current problems."

Alarmed, Roland said, "Oh no, I'll be—"

"The memo won't mention names, but I won't lie; it'll be obvious. There will be no threat to students of punishment or tattling. It'll appeal to their supposed good senses, which probably won't affect most of them. But perhaps it'll help others become more empathetic."

After a long pause, Roland said, "Maybe I should just quit the job. I'm making things worse."

"I don't want that to happen, son. I thought about cutting back to two days a week until things …"

Roland felt tears welling in his eyes. He turned away. "Dr. Sandberg, I'm afraid I'm so tired now, I can't think straight. Can we talk again on Friday?"

"Of course. You've had a lot to absorb. Hope you can relax some on your day off tomorrow."

• • •

When he returned to his work table, Roland unlocked his cabinet drawer, pretending to put a file inside. He looked over his shoulder before carefully slipping the knife into his pocket. He usually carried it to and from work, but given the present circumstances, it may be a good idea to have it at all times.

He made a mental note to call Jasper tonight and give him the latest details. His friend would have heard about the tribal council. Word had spread all over town, no doubt including the gas station where Jasper changed tires.

• • •

Quitting time finally rolled around, and Roland walked stealthily down the hall to the exit. He was almost out the door when Nancy appeared. Was she waiting for him?

"Roland, hi. I hope you're surviving the council's coming to town." She wore a lighter-weight jacket than the usual red parka.

"Barely." He was sick and tired of the questions, but Nancy had always treated him with respect and compassion.

"Well, I heard about the demands on Knox and the college, which was too bad. Things would certainly turn out worse for you."

"I know," Roland said, inching toward the door. "I was told there will be a memo sent out to not harass anyone. Anyone being me, of course."

"Really? I didn't hear that part. How would that work?"

Roland repeated what he'd heard from Sandberg. "So, thanks, Nancy, but I need to go. Got tomorrow off, thank God."

They said their goodbyes, and Roland sped out the door to Moose's waiting car.

Now he'd have a day to decide whether to work two days a week or just quit the damn place altogether.

CHAPTER 37

Nancy
Wednesday

Pretending to wait for a ride, I had purposely hung around the same door where I'd run into Roland before. I wanted to see how he was doing in light of the tribal men coming to town. I was afraid he'd quit or get fired for his own good. What a mess. All because the prejudice in this town, once spoken behind closed doors, exploded into the open. Even before Roland was unjustly accused.

I waited in Peggy's office for a ride to her place. I should walk, like Peggy did sometimes. Fresh air would clear my head, and pain receded in my back in warmer weather. By now, her apartment felt like a second home, with no stress for me anyway, except the stairs. We lived in close quarters, but the arrangement was working out. I hoped Peg felt the same.

Later, we made ourselves comfortable on the sofa with our customary gin and tonic, Ritz crackers, and cigarettes at the ready.

"Thanks for buying the gin, Nance." Peggy stirred her drink with a swizzle stick. "Sure is nice to come home to."

"Glad to contribute to the grocery bill. We need a proper happy hour, especially these days." Lucky for me, Mom slipped me ten bucks when I stopped in last weekend. Guilt still flickered on my mind, but never stayed too long.

"By the way, I ran into Roland on my way to meet you." I lit a Winston and savored the instant relaxation. For the hundredth time, I'd quit one of these days.

"That's happened a lot. Do you lie in wait for him?"

I knew Peggy was kidding. I played along. "Well, you know I have a soft spot for the guy. Anyway, he'd talked to Dr. Will, and Knox is sending a memo to everyone trying to smooth the tribal feathers."

"Yeah, I knew that. Heard it in the office just before we left today. It should go out tomorrow."

I took another swig of gin, and we continued to commiserate on the absurdity of expecting students not to say derogatory statements within earshot of others.

"I'm sure Knox will ask some other administrator to compose the message, and he'll need to approve it. "Peggy waited a beat. "Or maybe a scholarly English major like you should compose it, Nance."

I laughed. "Right. I'd tell the kids there's a new rule. If they can't say something nice, don't say it at all or they'll get suspended. That would work like a charm."

•　•　•

Later in the evening, I craved fresh air. The usual fog of smoke hung in the room, and Peggy liked to keep the windows closed in winter. Tempted to step outdoors and pace down the sidewalk, the thought of maneuvering the stairs was too much. Maybe tomorrow evening.

So, I worked on an assignment at the kitchen table, and Peggy sprawled on the couch reading *Lolita*. I'd mentioned that the tale of forbidden love and lust was causing a stir in the literary world, which piqued her sudden interest in Russian literature.

When the telephone jingled, she said, "I'll get it. You keep working."

Peggy spoke in a soft, muddled voice, but I was eager to hear her words. Not wanting to appear nosy, I stayed put.

About ten minutes later, I heard her hang up. Stepping into the kitchen, she said, "Sorry to interrupt you, but—"

"That's okay. Is there a problem?"

"Well, yes and no." Peggy sat across from me. "That was Judy all upset. Wait till you hear this." Peg's voice raised a pitch. "Loreen went AWOL. She's gone!"

"Gone where? Left home?" I asked in surprise. "What happened?"

Peggy took a deep breath. "Let me think a minute. Get this straight." She pulled her hair back in a temporary pony tail. "Dr. Will kinda kicked her out. The fight was over her prejudice against the Indians, Roland in particular. She knew about the tribal council and their demands, especially telling the cops to take Roland off the suspect list. And going to Knox wanting a rule about the kids heckling Roland."

None of this came as a shock. They'd fought over the Indians when she stayed in the motel. "Wow! Does this mean Loreen's going to stay at the motel again?"

"No. She packed last night and took off this morning in Dave's car. She somehow arranged that. Anyway, Judy says Loreen's headed for Chicago to stay with her folks. The final straw was when she knew Will was in cahoots with his boss Charlie to let Roland stay and not fire him. Said the Indian had ruined their lives by what he did, causing the fights between her and Will."

"Good God," I said.

"Then they both screamed at each other. She went off the deep end saying the Indians shouldn't be allowed to mingle with us or come into town or get welfare. They were an inferior race, on and on. Then Will yelled, called her a Nazi and said she could not live in the house with him and Judy."

I shook my head, still stunned. "I guess she can't kick him out. His job is here, and he'd have to hide it from his colleagues."

We finally ended the conversation and were ready to read until bedtime. I wondered if I should call Judy, but decided she was out of mental strength.

Images of childhood, three girls frolicking inside and outside the Sandbergs' house. Halcyon days of endless dinners, snacks, picnics, all beginning in kindergarten. Dr. Will, gentle, easygoing, his fatherly smile. I couldn't imagine him raising his voice to Loreen or anyone else. Her, I could believe flying off the handle, all her bigotry and conceit coming to a fiery head.

Perhaps Loreen's covert prejudices rose to the surface because of Barbara's death. Next thing, she'd be blaming Barbara for the demise of her family.

It seemed the townsfolk and the town itself had been split down the middle. Or three quarters. Some blaming the Indians. Others holding onto their opinions.

Last month, we had gone about our everyday business.

Then, all had capsized.

CHAPTER 38

Roland
Friday

This was the day. Roland had made his decision. He'd inform Charlie and Sandberg whether he'd quit his job or stay on for two days a week. Yesterday, he'd driven home to the reservation to escape the college and eat nourishing food. He was sick and tired of baloney sandwiches.

This morning they had met in Charlie's office. "Hi, kid, come on in." The boss seemed as jovial as ever.

Roland forced a smile and sat, while Charlie lit up a Chesterfield. Tempted to ask for one, Roland came to his senses and said nothing.

Will Sandberg knocked, and after a minute of social niceties, they got down to business.

Sandberg began. "We obviously want to hear your decision about cutting your hours, Roland. I'm sure you gave it careful thought." Roland noticed he hadn't mentioned the option of quitting altogether.

"Yes," Roland said. "I went home yesterday and talked about it a lot with my father and grandmother. She's always had common sense, but Pa sometimes lets his feelings take over." Roland brushed his fly-away hair from his forehead. "Anyway, I'd like to cut back to two days a week, and then maybe one. That is, depending what happens. If things get too bad, I think it would be best for you and the college if I quit either for good or maybe come back eventually."

Charlie and Sandberg listened without interruption. "That sounds good to me," Charlie said. "How about Tuesdays and Fridays?"

Roland shrugged and nodded his agreement.

"Fine. That's settled," said Sandberg. "By the way, the memo from Dr. Knox was distributed yesterday. I have a copy if you'd like to see it."

"Yes, I want to read it." Roland was curious, but uneasy as well.

Sandberg unfolded a sheet of paper from his side pocket and handed it to Roland. I need to hurry on, so keep it or pitch it. There's more where that came from."

"Thanks, Dr. Sandberg and Charlie. For everything." Roland took the paper and read several words.

"Read it at your table," Charlie said. "No hurry."

• • •

Roland finally found time to read the memo in semi-privacy later in the morning. It reflected the summarized version from Sandberg's words two days ago. Roland sped through the paper. At least his name wasn't on it, not that it would matter.

"Whew," he whispered to himself. "Thank God for that."

Reading the memo again, he squirmed at a couple phrases. *At an early age you all learned the immortal words of Thomas Jefferson stating that all men are created equal. At Eklund College everyone is to feel welcome and receive equal treatment.*

A brief history of the college followed, with glowing praise of its academic achievements. *In closing, we ask all of our students and staff to treat one another with kindness and respect. I do not want to hear of verbal bullying or loud remarks aimed at anyone.*

Knox finally signed off with hoping the campus environment will weather the present storm and triumph in the end.

Roland felt dazed. This official message all because of him. Knox may as well have asked the kids to lay off Roland Nightbird.

He'd show the memo to Jasper and perhaps his pa and Moose.

"Ready to help out in the auditorium?" Charlie interrupted his woolgathering.

"Sure." Roland folded the paper and stuffed it into his pants pocket right above the wadded-up bandana that hid the knife. A week ago, he'd begun carrying it with him during working hours, just in case.

On his way to the auditorium, Roland heard a couple muffled comments meant for him, but the speakers, rather than addressing him directly, looked straight ahead. He thought he recognized the jackasses from the heckling several days ago.

Later, when he'd finished his tasks, he and a couple other maintenance guys made their way down the hall toward their area. Roland noticed an unfamiliar young, skinny man striding toward them.

"Roland Nightbird?" the stranger asked as he approached the group. "Do you have a minute?" He wore a plaid, flannel shirt and carried a briefcase and wool jacket.

Suspicious, Roland glanced at his co-workers who gawked at the man, their faces blank.

"It's okay." The man's crooked smile complemented his sleazy appearance. "I'm Nathan Gill from the *Post*. If I could have a minute just to talk?"

"We gotta get back to our job," Larry said. Roland knew his pal was trying to protect him from the guy. He must be Nosy Nathan, the infamous reporter who took a dim view of Indians.

"Come on, let's get out of the way." Larry guided Roland's shoulder to the side as they continued on their way.

"I won't keep you longer than a couple minutes." Nathan's voice slithered as he leaned closer to Roland. "I just think—"

"We need to get back," Roland said, looking Nathan straight in the eye. "I have nothing to say to you." Proudly, he'd mustered up the guts to speak for himself.

"But—" Nathan started.

"Listen, pal," Curt, the other guy said. "We've been warned about you. If you write anything even hinting at Roland's name, you may be lookin' for another job."

"Really?" Nathan smirked.

"Yeah, really." Larry stepped toward him. "We'll be keeping an eye on your next columns, us and the higher-ups around here. People understand libel. We're not as dumb as we look."

With that, Roland and his two cohorts carried on, leaving Nosy Nathan to stew in his own juice.

CHAPTER 39

Nancy
Monday

At noon, I strolled home from classes to have lunch with Mom. I hadn't spoken with her for several days, so when she called yesterday, I thought lunch would be nice. My pa wouldn't be home from work; thank God he had a luncheon meeting to attend. I'd brought a small bag of laundry for Mom's pleasure that I'd stashed by Peggy's desk to avoid curious glances from classmates.

"Oh honey, it's good to see you." Mom wore her daily uniform, a drab housedress covered with an apron. With her warm brown eyes and soft Mamie Eisenhower bangs, she was an attractive lady, especially on Sundays, all gussied up for church.

I smelled the wistful aroma of roast beef as I followed her into the kitchen. We hugged, and I settled on my familiar kitchen chair.

"This is a special lunch just for you, Nancy." Mom lifted a pan from the oven and placed meat and other edibles onto two plates, which she carried to the table.

"You shouldn't wait on me, Mom, but yum! I haven't had sauerbraten for ages."

She beamed. "I planned ahead and made it for Sunday supper yesterday. Complete with German cabbage and mashed potatoes, just how you like it."

"Thanks. This is a real treat." I wished I could quit feeling so damn guilty about my sweet old ma. The subject of Pa was left unspoken.

"I know you're sick of talking about the Indian troubles, but what's the latest news?"

Mom took a sip of milk.

"Well, a little good news for Roland. The cops took him off the suspect list. The list of two, him and Albert."

"Really," Mom asked. "How did that happen?"

"Seems the Mayor and city council consented to meet the demands of the tribal group who wanted them to tell the cops not to consider Roland a suspect. They threatened a boycott if they didn't comply."

"Wow! That's something," Mom sat up straight. "A boycott of what?"

"The Thunder Lake tribe would refuse to do their banking in town, and they'd boycott stores and businesses. They do more shopping on the weekends than you might think. So, Mayor Rice decided it might hurt the owners when the tourists arrive in a few months." I took a minute to relish the tender meat and creamy potatoes. I never loved red cabbage, so I avoided it until the end.

"Hm." Mom dabbed at her mouth. "How interesting. How did you find all this out?"

"Peggy heard it through the office rumor mill, and then I sought out Will Sandberg to see if he knew for sure. He told me it's not an official announcement, but it's true. The mayor doesn't want to ruffle more of the Indians' feathers, so they're treading carefully." I took a nibble of cabbage.

"Will all that be in the newspaper?" Mom asked.

"Lord, no. Very touchy subject with Bruce McKee, the editor. He got flak for printing the article by that nosy reporter about reservation life. He almost fired the guy. So, the *Post* will stay clear of anything about the Indians."

When we finished our lunch, Mom said, "Now for dessert; your favorite. Apfelstrudel!"

My eyes lit up. "Oh, Mom, you shouldn't have gone to all this work, but I'm glad you did." She'd lovingly created her authentic German apple strudel from an old family recipe. I couldn't wait to savor the sweet, spiced apples, raisins, and flaky crust.

I was halfway through the strudel, trying not to gobble it, when I heard the front door open. Mom jumped up. "Gott im Himmel! He wasn't supposed to—"

"Clara, I'm home. Smells like you have lunch all ready—"

Mom rushed into the living room. "What are you doing here? I thought—"

"This is my house. Why wouldn't I be here? Anyway, it got canceled because … it's a long story. Let's have lunch."

Before Mom could stop him, Pa barged his way into the kitchen. His head jerked when he spotted me. "What the hell are you doing here? Come home to have lunch with your mama?"

It took monumental strength not to curse at him. Damn, he spoiled everything. "For your information, I thought you'd be gone, so I stopped in to see my one good parent."

"Why you … you ungrateful brat. I should've made you work your way through college instead of giving you everything on a silver plate." His chainsaw voice, thick in the air.

"That's a joke. You contributed a pittance for tuition and signed my student loans." However, I realized I was luckier than kids who worked and took out loans as well.

"Please, Theo, go in the living room and …" Mom's words lingered in the air.

"Why should I go?" his voice rose. "That girl is the—"

"Never mind, I'll leave. I refuse to stay another minute in this house with you around." I shoved back my chair and almost knocked it over as I stood.

"Good riddance," he jeered. "And give my regards to your pal, Injun' Joe."

I restrained myself from rising to his bait and turned to Mom for a hug. "I'm sorry, sweet ma. It'll be okay soon."

I gathered my coat and scrambled toward the front door. "I'll call you later."

Mom looked distraught. "Okay, honey. You come back tomorrow and get your laundry."

I hated to leave her there alone with that SOB. I'd dreamed of taking her away with me after graduation, or moving somewhere else with her and the younger kids, but she'd never agree. Afraid to manage on her own, along with her family's disapproval, and other reasons she'd conjure up, she'd stay put.

We all have our crosses to bear. Poor, dear Mom. What did she do to deserve her cross?

One thing I've learned at the ripe old age of twenty-two: I would never marry anyone who treated me like crap.

CHAPTER 40

Roland
Tuesday

Roland and his co-workers hurried back to their work station, grousing all the way about Nosy Nathan trying to manipulate Roland into an interview.

"You guys ready for lunch?" Charlie took a drag on his cigarette, then coughed.

"Those things'll kill ya," Curt said.

"I'm counting on it." Charlie harrumphed.

Curt and Larry told him about Roland and the annoying reporter.

"God, that guy's worse than … never mind," Charlie said. "You did a good job standing up to him. He can't mess with college kids. Probably thinks they don't have the guts to stand up for themselves." He turned to Roland.

"Remember, Roland, not one word to the reporters or the cops. They have nothing on you. No proof of anything."

"I'll keep doing that, boss. I've kept my head down all my life." He peeked inside his lunch bag. No baloney today. Moose had made him tuna fish sandwiches.

Roland grabbed a Coke from the break room and handed the student cashier a nickel. "Thanks, Roland," the kid said. "Hope things are going better for ya."

Surprised, he looked at the guy for the first time and wondered who he was. "Yeah, a little better. Thanks." At least one white kid treated him like a normal person.

Larry and Curt ate lunch in the break room, but Roland seldom socialized. He preferred to eat alone and brood in peace. He'd tucked the memo away in his cabinet to save for Jasper.

Charlie stopped by ten minutes later. "Some good news, kid. You're no longer a suspect. Bergstrom called earlier and said they have no official suspects as of now."

Roland put his sandwich down. "No kidding. What happened?"

"Seems your tribal pals told the cops they'd better lay off you or they'd boycott the town." Charlie gave a low laugh. "Wish I could've seen Bergstrom's face when the mayor told him to quit questioning you. Now, things should get better. See ya later." He whistled as he walked away.

Why did the tribal council have to come to town like men on the warpath? Roland's pa and council men should've pushed their anger aside and thought of Roland. What would their actions and threats do to him? Even that stupid memo made thing worse.

•   •   •

All afternoon the hands on the clock inched by at the pace of an iceberg. At 3:15, Roland threw his things together and was on his way. He made sure to say goodbye to Larry and Curt and thank them for helping with the Nosy Nathan business. Then he sought out Charlie and bid him farewell until Friday. Two days without working. The new schedule would take getting used to.

He reached the outside door and headed for the parking lot. Frosty air enveloped Roland as he stepped outside, and no one lingered at their cars to chat with friends. He planned to stop at

Jasper's for a beer and show him the memo. Although Jasper wasn't involved in the investigation, he should still keep up to date on things. You never knew when someone could ask him a casual question about his friendship with Roland.

He walked carefully since sidewalks, roads, and parking lots were partially slicked over. He headed past several cars and a pickup toward his old rattletrap.

Out of nowhere, he sensed an ominous presence.

"Roland. Gotta minute?" Albert Melowski appeared from the shadows and stood a couple feet away. Typical rich kid, a crooked smile but teeth like chiclets. He stood as tall as Roland, and may have outweighed him by twenty pounds or so. His remorseless blue eyes stared ahead, then scanned the surroundings.

Trying to clear his dry throat, Roland eyed Albert. "Got nothing to say." He stood his ground, determined to appear confident. Which he was, mostly.

"Hey, don't worry. Just a short, friendly conversation." Albert moved beside Roland and stood near a dented gray Plymouth, one car away from Roland's. "We'll try and stay out of sight."

"Don't want to talk. I gotta go." Roland turned toward his car.

"Your heap looks ready to fall apart," Albert taunted. "Be a damn shame if something happened to—"

"You threatening to wreck my car?" Roland's hackles skyrocketed. He wasn't taking this shit from a dumb jock like Melowski.

"Hold on, bud." Something flickered in Albert's eyes. Fear maybe? "Meant nothing by it." He lowered his voice, glanced around. "Look, Roland, I'm not owning up to being there, and I can't prove you were, so neither one of us … well, let's say we have each other by the balls. We both need to shut up to the cops and everyone else."

Roland had figured that out before, but he still didn't trust the big jerk. "Yeah, I wasn't there, so can't say anything about you. It's just that you're one of the guys goading people to accuse me, give me the stink eye, pick on me. And I'm getting damn sick and tired of it."

"No, man, I'm not—"

"Our people have been rejected for centuries, and there's just so much …" Reaching inside his pocket, he felt the handle of his knife. He slowly pulled it toward the opening of the pocket.

Albert jolted backward, his mouth dropping. "Whoa! No need for a fight. Just want an agreement."

Roland let the knife slip back to its hiding place. Albert must've seen the top of the handle, and figured what it was. "Agreement? What agreement could you give me?"

Albert's face muscles relaxed. "I'll tell the assholes to leave you alone. No more teasing or looks or anything. I'll tell 'em it'll be better for me. Haven't figured that out yet, but they're dumb enough to believe anything I say."

Roland hated and distrusted the guy, but Albert evidently feared Roland to some extent. "Yeah, like you can control people giving me a hard time?"

"It's all I can come up with right now."

Several students fired up their cars and backed out. Roland and Albert kept out of sight behind the gray pickup, but its owner could pop up any time.

"I better get going," Roland said.

Albert shifted his book bag to the other shoulder. "For the record, we never met or talked."

Roland grunted, turned to his old clunker, and opened the door. He looked back at Albert, who wandered off between the cars.

If he hadn't been wearing his bulky coat, Roland would have given himself a pat on the back for standing up to a white football hero.

At the moment, Albert was one less worry for Roland. Or was he?

CHAPTER 41

Roland
Tuesday afternoon

Driving to Jasper's house, Roland felt a sense of relief. He'd finally come face to face with Albert, something he'd been dreading. And it resulted in an uneasy truce.

Jasper's ma, Elsie, met Roland at the door. "Come on in, kid. Good to see ya." Her cigarette hung precariously from the edge of her mouth. "Just in time for some supper."

"Thanks, Elsie. Nice to feel welcome." Roland stepped into a cloud of smoke hovering in the living room. His mouth watered as he smelled hamburgers frying.

"Hi, bud," Jasper joined them from his basement room. "Food ready, Ma?"

Elsie sighed. "You better find a wife who's a good cook to wait on you hand and foot." She took a drag from her cigarette and turned to Roland. "I'm waiting for my adult sons to move out and give me some peace."

"Donny coming home tonight?" Jasper asked.

"Nah, your brother gave some reason for not coming, but I can't keep track of everything."

Roland suspected Donny stayed away to avoid seeing Roland. He'd always seemed warier of the Indians than Jasper and Elsie. Especially now that things had heated up for Roland.

Seated at the kitchen table, Elsie asked, "Life any better for you these days, kid?"

"Yeah, maybe." He told her and Jasper that he was no longer considered a suspect. "I guess the tribe coming to town helped that, but made it worse in some ways. More wise remarks from students. A bad atmosphere around there. Now I'm working only two days a week."

"Well, hell's bells." Elsie slammed her knife on the table. "I'd like to take those spoiled smart-mouthed little assholes and beat 'em up. They're a bunch of—"

"Settle down, Ma," Jasper said. "Nothing we can do."

"I know. I know, but it's so damn unfair. Roland's such a good guy. Just gets my dander up."

After supper, Jasper led Roland downstairs to his monastery of a bedroom. Jasper took a church key and popped the Grain Belts he'd taken from the refrigerator.

They flopped on the brothers' twin beds and guzzled their beer.

"Somethin' else happened yesterday," Roland said. "Ran into Albert, face to face."

"No shit." Jasper nearly dropped his beer can.

"Yeah, he was laying in wait for me in the parking lot. Said he just wanted to talk, not fight. Stayed outta sight. Don't think anyone saw us."

"What did he want?"

"It was kinda like a truce. We both knew neither one of us could say anything, but he wanted both of us to keep quiet about accusing each other. To make things easier on both of us with the cops and rumors." Roland realized how dumb that sounded.

Jasper twisted around on the bed as if uncomfortable. "Um, I didn't know whether to say this, but …"

"But what?"

"Some guys at work were talking about Barbara, kinda, you know, blaming the Indians. This guy asked me if I was pals with you, and I said I was, and that you wouldn't hurt a fly. Just gossip that's spread that ain't true."

"Crap, it never ends. Now you have to hear all that." Roland considered Jasper a loyal friend, but also afraid because he was at the scene that night too.

"Yeah, well," Jasper said. "I've been staying out of the boss's way. Hear he hates Indians. He could make up an excuse to fire me."

"Your imagination is running wild, but I know the feeling." Roland took a swig. "You're too good at the job, and you learn faster than those other guys put together. So, quit worrying. He won't can ya." Roland hoped he was right.

•   •   •

On the way to Thunder Lake, Roland worried more about Jasper's job and him putting up with comments, thinly disguised as dumping on Roland.

Willing himself to think of other things, Roland traveled along at a steady speed and dreamed up plans for staying in his old cubby hole of a house for a couple days.

Dinah was shaking out a rug on the front step as Roland turned in the driveway. She wore a tan wool sweater over the usual floral housedress and grinned when she spied Roland.

"Yer' a sight for sore eyes, boy." she gathered the rug into her arms. "Git' in here and sit."

Several minutes later, Roland settled himself in the parlor, blueberry baked dessert and coffee at the ready. Dinah parked in her usual ancient chair and began knitting a ski hat.

Soon, George Nightbird clomped in. "How goes the battle?" He spread his bulk on the couch, his beady fox eyes appearing suspicious.

"It's going," Roland answered, prepared for the same old conversation. "One thing is that I'm not an official suspect anymore, thanks to Jake and Red Horse."

"Good. At least that's something. Wondered if you knew yet." George sat straighter. "At least it's a small step to winning the war."

"Have ya thought more about quitting that job until all this is over?" Dinah asked.

"Nope. For now, it's two days a week." *When will people stop with the questions?*

She didn't let up. "It could get more dangerous around there. Every day. You'd be safer back here—"

"Ma, you've told him that a hundred times. Quit worrying over the boy. He's a grown man now."

"Don't you disrespect your mother, George. Or I'll tell the Wendigo monster where to find you."

George held his head with his hands as if holding it together. "Next you'll be saying the ghost of Sally Roy will capture me. What are we gonna do with you?"

Roland heard enough. He finished his dessert and took a final gulp of coffee. "It's been a long day, and I'm bushed." He stood and carried the cup and plate to the kitchen. "I need sleep. See you in the morning."

He said his good nights and made a beeline for his room and sank into bed ten minutes later. But his mind kept racing. How did the Chippewas become connected to Sally Roy's ghost? At least the legend of the Wendigo had been immersed in the north woods Chippewa culture for centuries. Nothing to do with white folks.

He'd been meaning to tell Jasper the myth of the monster sometime soon. Just for a speck of humor in this whole mess. Roland visualized his friend's face turning green when hearing the gory details of the north woods beast.

Smiling, he pulled up his blanket and drowsiness overtook him. Things were bound to get better, or he'd have to take a powder. Somewhere far away.

CHAPTER 42

Nancy
Thursday

Judy lived a short block from campus, so I stopped by her house on my way to class. I needed to borrow her copy of *Invisible Man* for a literature discussion. I think Roland would appreciate the book, but he might be self-conscious if I recommended it. Maybe if I knew him better.

"Come in, Nance," Judy greeted me at the door. Soldier yelped and jumped on my feet. "Got time for coffee?"

She handed me the book, and I stuffed it in my bag. We sat in the kitchen drinking coffee and chatting about classes and graduation. "At least I won't be teaching novels by Ellison in elementary school," Judy said.

"Good thing I like books." Only three more weeks, and I'd ditch this town for Green Earth.

"Have you talked to Roland lately?" Judy stirred more sugar in her coffee.

"No, I don't see him much since he only comes in two—"

The telephone jingled. "Wonder who that is?" Judy went to the kitchen wall and grabbed the receiver. "Hello?"

She pulled the long cord to the table. "Mom. How are you?"

Judy motioned me to lean in and listen, so I silently scooted next to her. She held the phone away from her ear so I could eavesdrop.

"Well, happy to report I'm just peachy. How's my Soldier boy? Sweet baby. I miss him so much."

"Your doggie's right here," Judy said. "Do you want to kiss him over the phone?"

"Don't be smart, young lady. Tell me, are you and your father still surviving without me? Who cooks and does laundry? Has Ida been showing up to clean?"

I cringed at the sound of Loreen's nasal, uppity voice. Judy glanced at me, rolling her eyes. "Yes, Mom, we've been doing fine without … I mean, we're managing. How are Grandma and Grandpa?"

After hearing about their health and how nice it was shopping at Marshall Field's and Carson Pirie Scott again, Judy asked, "Any plans to come home? I miss you, Mom."

"I miss you too, dear, but I don't know yet. By the way, Alma wrote that things aren't getting any better with the Indians up there. In fact, people all over Eklund are ready to protest, especially about the bunch who went on the warpath coming to town."

"For God's sake, that's ridiculous. Alma's really hitting the sauce it sounds like. Don't believe a word of that bull … baloney." Judy waited a second. "Actually, why is she writing you letters? I thought you didn't tell anyone you left."

"I'd told Alma I went to Chicago to help with Grandpa after his bout with pneumonia and didn't know when I'd return. The same story you were supposed to tell anyone who bothered to ask. Anyway, I had Alma's address and wrote her, and she sent me the news."

"Yeah, well, I need to get ready for class, so thanks for calling."

After they said their goodbyes, I drained my cup and stood. "I really need to go. Lucky you; don't have a class until later. See ya."

I didn't envy Judy putting up with Loreen. Thank God my mother was a kind, loving person.

• • •

Later in the day, Peggy and I treated ourselves to dinner at Jack's Diner downtown. We found a secluded table in the corner. I'd felt the urge to take a break from Peg's airless apartment and unwind. Grateful as I was for a place to stay, I often felt like a cloistered nun. Without the vow of silence.

Regrettably, I didn't date much, so no need for space to have a guy around. And Peggy's last boyfriend left two years ago, so the apartment had been adequate for one person. Maybe someday I'd meet someone, but not in this town.

"What looks good to you?" I asked as we read the menu. "I love their cheeseburgers."

"Think I'll order the chicken plate." Peggy shrugged out of her coat. She looked more weary than usual.

"Another boring day," I said as a pudgy blond waitress sidled over to us wearing a pink shirtwaist dress, tiny white apron, and clunky rubber-soled nurse's shoes.

"What can I get you ladies tonight?" She set two glasses on the table and poured ice water.

We placed our orders, and she waddled away. I began telling Peg about my day, but she sighed and fiddled with her napkin, folding it into smaller and smaller triangles.

"What is it, Peg? You look—"

"I know, I know." She stared a hole through me. "I've decided to tell you something I've never told anyone. I should've waited until after dinner, but there's never a good time."

"Jeez, Peg, you're scaring me." I had an idea what her secret involved, but I kept quiet.

"I'm sorry, but please just listen to me." She sipped her water. "You know about my childhood with my dad, but I've covered up things over the years. I loved Judy's dad and wished I had one like him."

I nodded, knowing firsthand what Peggy meant.

"In the last year, things have gotten worse with nightmares, memories, not eating … Dr. Norberg said sometimes trauma resurfaces after months or even years. Like men after the war coming back shellshocked. But the doc said it can happen to anyone who's been through a bad time, not just veterans. Anyway, I told him a few things about my old man beating us, but I didn't tell him everything."

"Oh, God," I murmured, guessing what was coming.

"Here you are, gals," the square-faced waitress chirped. She set our plates down. "More water?"

I shook my head, waved her off. She seemed to sense our desire for privacy and lumbered away.

Peggy took her fork and picked at her fried chicken. "I can't eat right now. Should've ordered a salad."

"It's okay. I'll start on my burger, and you go ahead." At least I wouldn't be staring her in the face.

She pulled back her pale yellow hair as if making a pony tail. "Well, you know having three older brothers was a good thing because someone was always around. Ma was mostly absent, not that she left, but her mind wasn't there. You know what I mean?"

"I think I do." I took another bite of cheeseburger, surprised I was hungry.

Peggy sipped her water and picked up a French fry. She nibbled on it, then put it down. "He was worse when he was drunk, waking us up at two o'clock in the morning to sweep the floor or take the trash out. Other times we'd get the strap." She stopped to rub her throat back and forth.

"Anyway, one night he dragged me into my bedroom and threw me on the bed. God knows what I'd done. I screamed and tried to kick at him, and next thing he was on top of me grabbing at my blouse. I … I felt his hands on me and … I heard my shirt rip." Peggy took a deep breath, her eyes turning watery.

"Jesus, Peg." I didn't want to hear more.

"And then I heard Paul holler. *Get up, you bastard! Get up or I'll shoot your goddamn head off!* It's still a blur, but pa grunted words I can't remember and managed to stand up and face Paul and his hunting rifle. *Put that down, you dumb asshole before ya — What, Pa? Kill you? Lay a hand on her again and I'll do it.* I don't remember much after that, but a week later I stayed with my cousin in Cass Lake until school started."

It took a while for Peggy's words to sink in. I reached for her hand, but she brushed it away. "No offense, Nance, but I just need to breathe now." She drained her water glass.

"What about Paul?" I asked.

"As the oldest brother, he'd gotten too big to hit. He was working by then, trying to save money to get out for good. We didn't talk about it for a long time, but I eventually thanked him. And the old man ever touched me again."

"I'm so sorry and angry this happened to you." I had a hundred more questions, but Peg looked worn to a frazzle.

"It happens, Nance. More than you think. You and Judy are lucky you were protected from scum of the earth like him."

"Yeah." My plate was almost empty, and Peggy's had barely been touched. "Let's blow this place, go home and have a good stiff drink."

Peggy smiled. "Thanks for listening. I feel a sense of relief, like a boulder has been lifted off my shoulders."

"Anytime." What else could I say?

Another first-hand lesson on the unfairness of life. Roland, and now Peggy. For different reasons, barriers awaited both at birth, causing more effort just to keep afloat. I was happy I could help a little.

CHAPTER 43

Roland
Friday

Roland wondered how much longer his life would circle in a holding pattern. Either the cops would arrest him or finally discover what really happened to Barbara Gruen. He felt bored and restless. Too many days off from work with little to do.

He left work for another long weekend, planning to meet Jasper before heading to the reservation. Driving south on Northlake Drive, he passed the iconic Paul Bunyan and the blue ox statues overlooking Spirit Lake. Then toward Cass Lake on Highway 2 which crossed a branch of the Mississippi where chunks of ice floated. Roland wished for the sun to emerge and banish the gloom.

Several minutes later, he pulled into the small, empty parking lot of Art's Hideaway, a sorry excuse for a local bar. Snow lay packed on the ground, and Roland shivered as he ambled up to the dilapidated place, its hinges hanging loose from a doorway featuring a rust-stained knob.

A musty odor greeted Roland as he stepped into the small, dim room.

A mammoth of a man sat behind the bar, his thinning gray hair hanging past his ears. "What can I get fer ya?" His voice wheezed. "Have a seat ... plenty of 'em." He chortled.

Roland wandered to a corner table and hoped the place wouldn't fill up with prying eyes. "I'll have a Grain Belt and a bag of Fritos." No hot food served here. He'd have to wait for a real dinner.

The big man brought beer and chips, limping along. "Man, it's April already. Still colder than a witch's ti--"

As if rehearsed, the door opened, and there stood Jasper. "Roland, good to see ya."

Jasper shrugged out of his parka as the barkeep took his order and hobbled off.

"Is the dump always this empty?" Roland opened his bag of chips and held it toward Jasper.

"Pretty much. But it's early yet. It livens up later at night. Picked it cuz it's safer than the Muni. People are worse about Indians right now." Jasper took a chip and chewed noisily.

"Yeah, I've heard this place is friendlier toward us because it's closer to Cass Lake." Roland took a gulp, figuring Jasper's drink would come any minute.

"Makes sense, mostly Indians live there."

"It's right on Leech Lake Reservation, so yeah…" Roland paused. "Well, everything okay at work? Boss fire you yet?"

"Nah. Like you said before, I'm too good." Jasper laughed at his own quip. "What's new with you?" He took a snort of beer the guy had set down.

"I talked with Pa and Moose about what I could do. A couple days ago, Pa tried to talk me into quitting the college and leaving home to get a job."

"Where?" asked Jasper.

"We got kin down in South Dakota. Lake Traverse. Pa said it's far away, about 250 miles. Some of the family live in Aberdeen in case I don't want to live on another reservation." Roland drained his bottle. "Ready for another one?"

The man had disappeared, and Roland tried to peek behind the counter and shelves of liquor. "Hey, mister, could we get another beer or can we —"

The guy shambled through a doorway. "Yeah, how 'bout more chips too?"

Roland asked for two bags of chips and salted peanuts, which arrived shortly.

"Why does your old man think you should go so far away? Lots of jobs in the Cities, especially Minneapolis. You could get trained as a mechanic, like me."

"Right." Roland didn't want to insult Jasper, but he wanted to have a professional job someday. "Pa says it's best for me to go far away where nobody's heard of the investigation, so not to suspect me of anything. Don't know where he gets that idea. My picture isn't in the newspapers, so how could they tell one Indian from another?"

"Come to think about it, you all kinda look alike. Hope ya don't mind me sayin'."

Roland snorted. "Nah, I'm used to insults. Anyway, I told Moose about me leaving when I came back yesterday from Pa's. And damned if Moose thinks the opposite."

"He wants you to stay put?" Jasper asked.

"Yup. He thinks it would be a mistake to give up that good college job. He says I got good people there looking out for me, people that can help me get ahead. Things will get better sooner or later, and I could go on and take some classes like Sandberg and the BIA man promised."

Jasper chewed on a handful of peanuts. "Jeez, I dunno. I can kinda see both sides. I guess running off might seem better now, but in the long run, you could get some college. I have an uncle who got an engineering degree on the GI bill after the war."

Jasper's comment made Roland think his friend may be smarter than he looked. "I think Moose wants me to live like a white man. Odd, because he's always hated them, but they do live better."

"Ha. Not all of 'em. Look at me."

They agreed that Jasper wasn't dirt poor, and was much luckier than Roland's people.

"Another thing, you have all those crazy-sounding myths and weird beliefs like different spirits and ghosts and ..." Jasper paused. "You know, like the ghost of Sally Roy and that win ... wona ... monster."

"I've been meaning to tell you the real story of the Wendigo monster."

"What's stopping you?"

Roland guzzled the last of his brew. "First thing, the legend started centuries ago by Chippewas. So, the Wendigo lives in the freezing cold, like here in northern Minnesota and Canada, carries the cold with him in the woods. The closer you get to it, the colder you get, and you can see your breath even in the summer."

Jasper fiddled with his empty bottle, twisting it around. He seemed bored.

"Anyway," Roland continued, "the creature is horrible-looking with hollow red eyes that glow, and its teeth are so big and jagged, they tear the skin around them. Plus, it kinda looks like a deer or other wild animal, but it stands fifteen feet tall and stalks around looking for people to eat. Its lips are all torn and bloody, and..." Roland noticed Jasper looked a little green around the gills.

"Wanna hear more?"

"Yeah." Jasper's voice unenthused.

"Well, the Wendigo stinks of decay and sewage people can smell a mile away. If you hear it screech, you lose consciousness. The main point is it's a cannibal, tearing someone to shreds while eating the ..."

"Enough, man. I got the point." Jasper put one arm through his parka.

"Wait. Don't go yet. You haven't heard the best—"

"I gotta go."

Roland guffawed. "Okay. Okay, I'll end it. No more blood and—"

"Shut up. I'm leavin'—"

Roland grabbed Jasper's arm. "Just kiddin'. Promise this is the end. The reason us Indian kids heard the story growing up is parents used it as a lesson, or threat. That you better not go roaming in the woods by yourself, especially after dark or the Wendigo will catch you and devour … well, you get the gist."

· · ·

Darkness surrounded Roland and Jasper as they stumbled into the parking lot. They stood, shivering as they talked of Roland's future plans.

As they headed toward their cars, Roland said, "By the way, do you know why the Wendigo's son got kicked out of school?"

Jasper paused, looking confused. "No, why?"

"He was caught buttering up the teacher."

"Asshole." Jasper shook his head and turned away.

Roland was still chuckling to himself as he wheeled out of town. The first time he'd laughed for days.

CHAPTER 44

Earl Krepp
400 Dalton Street, Eklund, Minnesota

Earl knew it was coming. The private conversation Albert Melowski would arrange because he'd discovered Earl was the witness. Just the two of them together in the large basement room Al had rented since junior year.

The same question still haunted Earl: how did he get himself into this mess? A mess that could change his life, and not for the better. He'd been at the party that night. Noticed Albert and his pals, who were glued to the football star at all times. Earl wasn't in Al's in-crowd. As an athlete, he'd never set the sports world on fire. Been on the sidelines all his life. Since freshman year, he was (in his own eyes) a tag-a-long, playing backup, rarely yet enthusiastically, for the Eklund Beavers.

Parking his dented-up Mercury in front of the two-story white house that included Al's campus home, Earl thought he'd rather be anywhere but here. Street lights shone on lawns and sidewalks carpeted in white from an unexpected snowfall two days ago. He breathed in a smell of firewood in the frigid air.

He trudged up the sidewalk and around to the back door, its porch light beaming an ominous welcome. According to Al, the owners were gone, so the door would be unlocked.

Earl jiggled the knob and cautiously entered a landing which led to the basement stairs.

"Al? I'm here," Earl called, clutching his brown paper bag containing a pint of rum he'd bought at the Muni.

"Come on," a voice yelled back.

When Earl stepped into the downstairs room, it seemed Al was progressing well on his highball.

"Nothin' like whiskey on the rocks. Mix your poison, ol' pal, and come relax."

Earl made a rum and Coke in the kitchenette and then sank into a worn easy chair. Al sprawled on a brown upholstered couch, glass in hand. A bottle of Grain Belt sat on the coffee table beside a bag of Fritos.

"First time you've been here?" Al asked as if he didn't know.

"Yeah, pretty nice." Earl swirled his glass. "You got lots of space. More than mine for sure." He took in two open doors, obviously a bedroom and bathroom.

They shot the breeze and drank for the next twenty minutes or so, Al leading the conversation. Earl felt antsy, wanting to get down to brass tacks. Enough football, graduation, and career plans.

Al took a swig of beer as a whiskey chaser. "Man, I'm gonna be three sheets to the wind pretty soon. Lost count of these." He held up his half-empty glass.

Earl said nothing. He had been secretly watering down his drinks, his back to Al. The last time, he'd only poured Coke in the glass. He wanted to stay alert just in case things got ... he wasn't sure what.

"You know, man, been doing a lot of thinking about stuff, and this Barbara mess is really wrecking my life. And we know what it could do to our future if things turn ... well, worse." Al took a fist full of chips and smacked them loudly.

Earl stiffened in his chair. "Yeah?"

"Well, Earl, ol' buddy. Word leaked that you're the cops' eyewitness to that night. Seeing me and the Injun. Only me and a few others know. That's all I'll say about that." Al gulped his drink. "But your name will spill out more sometime. Can't keep stuff like that hidden forever."

"I suppose." Earl wasn't stupid. He knew that. He just hoped his name would stay under wraps until graduation. Then he'd go somewhere far away and find a job.

"So…" Al paused. "I'm gonna ask you a big favor." Another pause. "I want you and me, or just you, to tell the Bergstrom cop that you might have been mistaken that night— "

"What?" Earl's impulse took over. But he cautioned himself.

"Just hear me out." Al put down his glass and leaned forward. "You know, some people say it was dark and a blizzard, and how could you see who was there? Maybe your eyes aren't that good."

"Yeah, the cops asked that too. Thought if I wore glasses, they'd fog up outside. Asked if I'd take an eye test. I've always had good vision, so that wasn't a problem."

Al shrugged. "The point is, I want my name removed as a suspect. So, if you tell them you aren't sure anymore and have thought about it, blah blah blah, you don't want to blame a … how you say, an innocent person."

Earl's mouth dried up. "I don't know, Al. Let me think on it."

"Okay, five minutes."

Was Al kidding? "I need more than that. I thought a day or two."

"Won't do, buddy. I need to get it done pronto before my resumes are due in. We need to make plans tonight." Al stood. "I gotta take a leak. Think on it then."

Earl had always wanted the truth. So had everyone else. Maybe if he made a deal with Al, like getting an honest answer to what Al ready did that night … Nah, he'd just lie. But if he promised Al he would renege his witness statement, and Al's story wasn't glossed over. Oh, hell, he'd try it. Al might be drunk enough for the truth to spill out.

• • •

Sometime later, Albert Melowski readied himself to uphold his end of the bargain Earl had proposed.

"All right, here goes." His words sounded like he talked with a mouthful of mush. "I was at the party maybe an hour or so. Don't know what time. Prob'ly around nine or so I got there."

Earl nodded, saying nothing.

"You've heard about the kids who saw me there. The cops questioned everybody there. A few said I was talking to the girl, getting fresh. Maybe I was. Things were slowing down. Boring party. I was ready to leave anyway."

Al drank his beer and wrinkled his nose. "God, it's warm. Tastes like piss." He stood, staggered to the sink and dumped the rest down the drain. Opening the refrigerator door, he asked, "Want a cold one?"

"Nah, I'll stick to mine here." Earl lifted his Coke to his mouth and pretended to drink.

Al returned. "Wasn't my caliber of parties, but me and the guys went for something to do. I was on my own … girlfriend went home for the weekend. So, here's this cute little girl looking lost. Don't remember seeing her before. Probably a freshman. Sitting alone, parka on her lap. Don't know what I said, the usual flirting, ya know."

Earl didn't know. Not an expert at flirting.

Al slurred on. "I found out Barbara was her name. Heard the next day she was Dave's little sister. Jesus God, what a shock that was."

Earl did not respond.

"Then she tried to stand up, holding a Coke bottle and fiddling with the parka. I said, 'Hey, where ya going?' She mumbled something about her friends and leaving the party. Maybe she'd never been to a party before, but there was something kinda ... um, nice and innocent about her, ya know?"

Earl, not sure, again kept quiet.

After another chug of chilled beer, Al slouched backward, dumped his stocking feet on the coffee table. "I told her to let her hair down, have some fun, but she was determined to leave. She wandered into another room, so I started shooting the bull with some other kids. Then, who knows when, there she was, going out the back door. I waited a few minutes, then took my jacket from the pile in the bedroom and slowly made my way toward the door where she'd left. I wanted to sneak away, not to make a big deal— "

The phone rang. Al glanced at the wall clock. "Jeez, who's calling this late? Probably Anne."

He answered, then pulled the cord into his bedroom. "I'll only be a couple minutes."

Earl waited impatiently while a couple minutes ticked into fifteen.

"Sorry, that was Anne. Had to tell me everything about ... ah, never mind." Al leaned back on the couch. "Let's see, I think I left off when I ditched the party. Freezin' ass cold out, blizzard worse. Walked along toward campus, but the road was kinda disappearing in the snow ... "

Al's voice droned on. He'd slogged along the path, thinking maybe the girl had left right behind friends he hadn't seen and she was home by now. Then he saw her ahead. Who else could it be? She was slowing down, staggering, veering off to the left, then disappeared into a flurry of blinding snow. He caught up to where he thought she'd disappeared but at first saw nothing. After yelling her name and turning every which way, he spotted something dark. He bent down, tried to brush the swirling snow away, only to see part of a huge tree trunk.

At one point, Earl stood and headed for the bathroom. When he came out, Al was splayed out on the sofa, eyes shut, wheezing.

"Wake up. I gotta go soon. It's getting late." Earl wanted to hear the end of the story, even though being with Al made his skin crawl.

"Huh?" Al yawned, groaning. After a couple attempts, the big guy managed to sit.

He really was a disgusting son of a bitch, and Earl regretted ever letting himself get involved with him.

Al wiped off drool trickling down his chin. "Well, to wrap up the story, the girl had found a little shelter under some thick limbs on the trunk and … um, everything's kind of blank. Her furry hood was on her head. A scarf too, I think. She looked right at me, noises coming from her mouth."

Earl's stomach lurched. "You mean she was alive when you found her?"

"Yeah, uh … I bent close to her face and … and said I was gonna help. Wind wasn't as bad hunched on the ground." Al stopped, seemed to think. "I was drunk, I admit it. I just wanted a little kiss, maybe a feel, but she still wouldn't … wouldn't …"

"Jesus, stop!" Earl stood, took one step to Al and grabbed him by the neck. "You … you left her there to die. You tried to suffocate her when she … she … what did she do? Tell you to leave her alone? Even in a blizzard, you couldn't get her to … "

"Wait. Wait, Earl. I'm in the bag. Drunk too much. That's not what happened. You got it all wrong … said I was gonna get help." He shoved Earl's hands away from his neck and tried to stand. "We had a deal. You gotta tell the big cop. You promised if I'd — "

"To hell with our deal," Earl raged. "You killed her, you miserable piece of shit." He grabbed his parka from the chair and headed for the door. Al's story was full of holes, but he never denied leaving her there. And who else could've smothered her?

In a flash, Al sprang to his side. "You're not going anywhere, ya pansy ass. Stay right here until— "

A surge of adrenaline erupted in Earl's entire body, and with a strength he'd never mustered before, he faced Al head on. Grasping his upper arms, Earl shoved Al to the floor. The big jerk lay there in a daze lasting several seconds.

Earl seized his parka. He was out the door and into his car, his impulse screaming at him to get the hell out of there.

Terrified of what Al might do, Earl headed toward Walker, where his cousin Gordy lived.

In the morning, he'd come up with a plan, but what the hell would he do?

CHAPTER 45

Earl
Sunday

The previous night when Earl had tapped on Gordy's bedroom window, he'd hoped he wouldn't disturb the whole family. Luckily, his cousin crept to the window and peeked out the curtains. After motioning Earl to come in, they sat in the living room in the semi-darkness. Earl gave Gordy a general explanation of the situation. Then, seeing he was too exhausted to go on, Gordy urged him to flop on the sofa and sleep.

• • •

At ten o'clock Sunday morning, Earl and Gordy sat in a corner diner near Leech Lake in the scenic resort town of Walker, about twenty miles from Eklund. Earl wolfed down peppery sausage, fried eggs, oatmeal, and several cups of black coffee. Between bites, he and Gordy discussed Earl's next step. Gordy, a reliable family man in his thirties, offered common-sense and realistic options.

By noon, Earl was driving back to Eklund. Swollen gray clouds hovered in the sky, and patches of icy snow dotted the narrow road. Another gloomy day, but he felt a modicum of relief now that he'd made a plan.

However, details of yesterday's meeting with Al kept swirling around in his mind. At least now, after a few hours of sleep and the talk with Gordy, Earl knew what he had to do.

• • •

That evening, he finished a meal of Swanson turkey dinner and a Coke. At last, it was all over for him. At least the hard part.

Several hours earlier, Earl had forced himself to walk into the police station, where he asked to see Officer Bergstrom. The cop had the day off, but his partner, Nysen, was available to see Earl.

They met in a small walled-off cubicle with a plain metal desk and two chairs. After he told Nysen the gist of the story, the cop made a phone call.

Ten minutes later, Bergstrom joined them. He plopped his wide frame into a chair. *This better be good. You spoiled my Sunday poker game with the boys.*

Both cops had listened intently while Earl told them everything he could remember from yesterday, especially details Al had revealed toward the end. Difficult as it was, Earl repeated Al's account of how he'd left Barbara in the snow.

I think he couldn't face a girl rejecting him, not even when she's half dead. He must've tried to smother her with his bare hand or maybe with gloves on. Maybe she screamed, but who'd hear that in a blizzard? Earl tried to sound objective, but it was damn hard.

Bergstrom noted Earl's assessment, but lamented the lack of hard evidence. Just hearsay.

The cops advised Earl not to breathe a word of their meeting to anyone. Even close family, friends, or college staff. Nysen said to keep a low profile and avoid Albert as much as possible. Of course, Al would want to know whether Earl had asked the cops to rescind his witness statement. But in the light of day, he was no longer afraid of Al. After all, now the cops knew what Al did.

Shifting back to the present, he put his dishes in the sink to wash later. His roommate was still away for the weekend, giving Earl more time to think. He knew Al would lie in wait for him, and Earl planned to fib, saying he kept his promise to rescind, but didn't know what the cops decided. It was out of Earl's hands, and he'd tell Al they shouldn't be seen together just in case. In case of what, he didn't know, but it sounded good to him.

But two questions would continue to plague Earl:

Would Barbara Gruen eventually receive justice?

And would Albert Melowski ever pay for his crime?

CHAPTER 46

Nancy
Monday

I sat in Peggy's living room waiting for her to leave for an office Tupperware party.

"It's not too late to come, Nance. We can bring a guest, like I've said a hundred times." Peg checked herself in the mirror by the door. "How do you like my new lipstick color? Audrey Hepburn wore it in *Sabrina*."

"Looks good on you. The red brings out your hair and eyes, even though Audrey's a brunette." She seemed perkier.

"What about the party?" Peg blotted her lips with a Kleenex.

"Nah, thanks, I'm still gonna pass. I have reading to do, and I'm not ready for Tupperware yet."

After Peggy left, I breathed in my solitude. I'd felt at loose ends for several days with the investigation stagnating. Were people losing interest in Barbara's case? Even Judy's mind was on other things, like planning her wedding, although Dave wanted to wait until the case was resolved. *I told him that could take forever, and he sort of accused me of not caring about Barbara. Maybe I should hold off booking Miss Hagen to sew my wedding dress. Oh, Nancy, what should I do?* I had no mental energy to worry about Judy's wedding decisions.

All these problems. I was still reeling from the secret Peggy had kept for years. Poor girl. I hoped her old man rotted in hell. Like Peggy, I guess we all hide our shame behind a curtain of something: drinking, overeating, not eating, smiling. The list goes on. To paraphrase Shakespeare, we're all actors in a play.

However, one bright spot lay ahead. In two weeks, I'd be in Green Earth, teaching eager students the joys of Byron and Keats. Oh yes, and Shelley too.

Mom had arranged for old Mr. Griebel from church to lend me his worn-out Nash to drive back and forth on weekends. Dave promised to check out the car since my father was out of the picture and not speaking to me.

I went to Peg's bedroom to open my suitcase. I rifled through my underwear, pajamas, and extra blouses. I had hidden Barbara's diary under a bunch of Kotex pads, and I decided to read it after all this time. I didn't know why. I guess my curiosity got the best of me. Also, it occurred to me I might find a clue to help the investigation, like a friend nobody knew about or something that had happened to Barbara. Could I get in trouble for withholding evidence? Something else I thought of too late. I willed myself to accept the reality of my decision.

Settled back on the couch, I smoothed my hand over the small, leathery journal, then slowly opening the pages, I began to read.

I've been back for my sophomore year a week now, and things are about the same as last year. I haven't seen Him yet, but I'm hoping to meet again. I won't say his name in case this journal falls into the wrong hands, but from now on I'll call him He or Him. First of all, my class schedule is…

I skimmed the next pages where she described her courses, professors, roommate, and several friends. I had a vague impression that Barbara was lonely and sensitive, but I don't know why. I turned to the next page, dated September 21.

I'm so happy! He saw me in the hall and smiled at me. I love the small gap between his teeth. His black hair looked trimmed, he's so big and handsome. He came toward me and whispered can you be there at three? He meant our secret spot from last year outside the music room that had an enclosed space down the hallway. I could hardly concentrate on my world history class, waiting to talk to him again.

The time finally came, and my heart was thumping when I saw him standing there. We looked around and snuck down the hall and around the corner. He said I looked as pretty as ever, and he missed seeing me over the summer. I said the same things, and I felt the same wonderful feelings as last year. We talked about meeting somewhere outside campus some late afternoon, but couldn't figure out anything. We both said what a shame it was we had to sneak around.

My mouth felt like sawdust. I put the diary aside, poured a glass of water, and gulped it down. I needed a breather. Who was *He*? Why sneak around? I picked up the diary and continued where I'd left off.

It's been a long time since I wrote last. The history class is really tough, lots of reading and notes. But He and I met a few times, and once we snuck down to the lake and sat on a bench and talked. Nobody else around, and we don't walk close together. I finally found a guy I can really talk to. He's not really a college guy though, more like a man. He has the kindest eyes and He likes to hear about my growing-up years and my classes. I want to kiss him, but maybe next time we meet it'll happen.

I kept reading, but no new details on her heartthrob. I pictured her heart-shaped face and dainty pink mouth. I needed a break, so I went to the kitchen for cookies and lukewarm coffee.

A few minutes later, I picked up the diary, hoping for information to use in finding her. I couldn't bring myself to even think of the horrible word.

I no sooner opened the pages when I heard the front door slam, then feet hurrying up the stairs. Damn, why was Peggy home so early? I snapped the diary shut and scrambled to the bedroom. I returned the diary to its rightful place in the suitcase. Peggy came through the door as I sat down.

"You're early. Party no fun?" I opened my textbook.

Peg looked at her watch. "It's been over an hour." She took off her coat. "But yeah, I left before it was finished. I was bored to death, so after I'd ordered the cheapest thing there, I begged off. Told 'em I had a headache."

Of course, I hadn't told a soul about the diary, even though I was bursting at the seams to tell Peggy. I would read the rest another time.

Wednesday afternoon

That *another time* came on Wednesday. Peggy was still at work. I retrieved the diary from its hiding place, settled on the couch and thumbed through the pages, hoping to learn more about *Him*.

October 5 – I feel like I'm walking on air! We had our first kiss over a week ago, and it was wonderful!! I'd never really kissed a boy before, other than a spin the bottle game in junior high and another time on a blind date in high school. But they didn't count… cuz they were only once and I didn't even know the boys. Anyway, His lips look so soft and he's so kind. He understands me, and I feel like my life is worth living.

In the next part, Barbara wrote more details on daily routine and classes. She liked her course in American literature, especially Emily Dickinson's work. She quoted a stanza from "I'm Nobody" and I felt myself tearing up. Also, she could relate to the poet's personal life growing up burdened by a strict father and loneliness. I've always been amazed that Dickinson wrote so eloquently with such insight considering her reclusiveness.

I quit waxing poetic and went on reading.

The other day I met Judy for coffee in the student union, and she said she and Dave are quite serious. Dave always had more friends than me. He has a much better personality. So Judy said she hoped he'd propose at Christmas or Valentine's Day. I really wanted to tell her about Him, but I just couldn't. Judy might be my future sister-in-law if she snags Dave, but I don't know her well enough to tell her yet. Maybe sometime.

The following pages contained typical college-girl ramblings about Christmas plans and the new year, how Barbara couldn't believe it was nearly 1955. She mentioned Him now and then, but nothing new. She knew what it felt like to be in love, and as I read, I loved vicariously through her words. How innocent she was.

I skimmed ahead to February, a couple weeks before the fateful party.

He and I talked a little about our future. Just plans for the next few months – it's getting so hard to keep sneaking around. But maybe it would help by telling somebody we trusted and get some advice about not hiding anymore. I don't know who we'd talk to. Somebody older who is kind. Not my parents, I could never do that. Judy's dad, Dr. Sandberg is so nice and he'd be perfect, but I don't have the courage yet.

I looked up from my reading. I was getting close to the end. Did I really want to read the rest of what was Barbara's life? Yes and no.

Glancing at the clock, I guessed Peggy wouldn't be home for another half hour, so I grabbed a Coke from the fridge and settled on the sofa bed. I stared at the cover of the diary and opened it where I'd left off.

Barbara wrote that her roomie, Joyce, was talking about the coming weekend when Diane across the hall knocked and came in their room. She yakked on about her test grades in chemistry and other stuff, and then she told them about a party on Friday night. She heard about it from a senior Barbara didn't know. Diane said it would be off campus in a rented house and urged them to attend. The weather was terrible, but it was close enough to walk. They didn't have a car anyway.

Joyce and Diane were excited to go. We hadn't been to an off-campus party with alcohol. They snuck beer when they could, but I never liked liquor of any kind. They begged me to go with them. I'm not sure why because I'm so quiet and hate to dance and do stuff like normal girls. So, this morning of the party, Joyce said that some other girls from our floor were going to that stupid party and I really should come along. She said it would be good for me to get out with other kids and maybe make new friends. And who knows? Even meet a boy. I wanted to say I already have someone. But I told her I'd think about going, just to shut her up.

Thinking I'd reached the end because the page was only half filled, I flipped through the rest of the book until I discovered more.

I probably shouldn't write the secret, but maybe because it's at the end, nobody would bother if they accidentally found this. So, we first met last year in April, just catching each others eye in the hall. Something about his eyes. Maybe most kids wouldn't bother looking at him twice, but I saw something sad, but nice in his face. The next couple months of school, we met a few times, secretly of course. After all, he was older and… well, you know. We both knew there was no future for us, not ever probably. Unless big changes would come in people's minds and in the world, I guess.

I have so many feelings about us, but the truth is loving Him is such sweet sorrow, which I borrowed from Romeo and Juliet except those lovers were parting. I feel both happy and tearful at the same time. And even if we can't end up together in years to come, I'm so thankful I found Him and could become a happy person. He said we were two lonely spirits who found each other. And I treasure the picture of the eagle taped on the next page. Someone in his family drew it.

I turned the page and there sat a pen and ink drawing of a proud eagle perched on a branch. Barbara had apparently drawn the outline of a heart beside its beak.

You said the eagle is the symbol of love in your teachings because it has a connection to the Creator. The eagle has the strength to fly higher in the sky than other creatures, putting it closest to the Creator in the heavens.

Several lines below the picture Barbara wrote her final words.

I gasped out loud, my right hand flew to my head. "Oh, God. Oh, God, it can't be."

• • •

I'll always love you, Roland.

CHAPTER 47

Nancy
Wednesday

I froze, shell-shocked. How could that be? The diary fell from my hands onto my lap, closing silently. How did they meet? I reread it to make sense out of it. Roland was an Indian. Mixed race couples were taboo. Maybe illegal. And he's older. Well, a few years. My thoughts raced around like a moth trapped in a lamp.

When I heard Peggy on the stairs, I stashed the diary between the cushions. She opened the door. "Ready for happy hour?" She hung up her wool coat.

"Oh, really, well I …" Words eluded me.

Peggy kicked off her boots and sank into the couch. "Hope it doesn't snow anymore. I'm ready to ditch these boots." She paused, eying me. "You seem jumpy or something, Nance."

"Do I?" I forced a weak laugh, fiddling with my wristwatch. "Guess I'm just distracted. You know, the investigation, my teaching."

"You've said that a dozen times. Anything else bothering you?"

"No, don't worry." I was dying to tell Peggy what I'd read, but of course, I couldn't. I should probably turn the diary over to the cops, but Roland would be ruined. They'd accuse him of wrongdoing, and Al would deny he'd been there to save himself. Not to mention, I'd be accused of stealing the diary. No turning back. The die was cast.

"Okay. Well, I'll go mix us a drink."

I snuck the diary away and returned it to its rightful place under the Kotex. For whatever reason, I thought Barbara may get a laugh out of where I hid it.

After a dinner of Peggy's concocted meatloaf, we passed the evening with small talk, reading, and a couple games of cribbage.

Lying wide awake in bed, I puzzled more over Barbara's revelation. I still couldn't comprehend the situation. I wondered if I should show it to Roland and whether he had a right to read Barbara's last hopes and dreams.

Eventually, I decided Roland had more of a right than I did to see the diary. But when would be the right time? I'd be gone in a week to Green Earth and would only come home on weekends when Roland wouldn't be around.

Seemed like next week would have to be the time. If I could muster up the courage.

I'd also need to dream up a place we could meet. Someplace out of the way where we could have privacy.

But where?

CHAPTER 48

Roland
Friday

On his way to work Friday morning, the realization hit Roland that Barbara had gone to the Other Side Camp, as his ancestors would say, exactly seven weeks ago. However, it was an ordinary day to most folks. Things at the college seemed to quiet down, with fewer stares and whispers his way. Had the cops given up their search?

Oddly enough, it hadn't been too difficult for Roland to keep his painful secret buried. He'd faked his way through everyday conversation all these weeks, other than getting tongue-tied when the cops questioned him.

He wound his way around the parking lot and found a slot on the far side to hide his jalopy. The ground was mostly gravel and dirt, now that the temperature had soared to forty degrees, more like a typical April day. The familiar aroma of woodsmoke and crisp air reminded Roland of his home on the reservation.

He no longer wore gloves or scarves, especially the infamous Chippewa scarf that could've caused his arrest. He ambled along between dusty, dirty cars until a deep gravel voice behind him interrupted his thoughts.

"Haven't seen you for a while." Albert stepped beside Roland. "Everything okay?"

Roland gave him an icy stare. "What do you want?" He kept shuffling toward the building.

"Just wondering if you'd heard anything new about … well, you know." His granite jaw jutted forward as he tried to block Roland's path.

"I'm not talkin' to you." Roland stopped, took in Al's steel-blue eyes. "Don't bother me again." Roland paused, kept staring, and marched away.

He felt a surge of confidence as he entered the building and arrived at his workplace.

Maybe he could let his guard down, but then thought better of it. Don't get too smug. Things can always go south.

"Roland, good to see ya," Charlie strode in, holding a Chesterfield between yellowed fingers. "Things have been pretty quiet around here. Let's hope they stay that way."

Roland hung up his jacket as he breathed in the tempting aroma of the cigarette. "Nothing new from the cops, I guess."

"Not a word," Charlie answered. "I wouldn't be surprised if they closed the case one of these days."

On the one hand, Roland would sigh with relief at the idea, but then Albert would go free, and Barbara … well, what about justice?

Later in the day, Roland headed for the admissions office to fix a leak in the ceiling when he ran into Nancy.

"Oh, hi, Roland." She seemed oddly surprised to see him, almost like she preferred to avoid him. Her smile was friendly as usual, but something seemed missing. She hitched up her bookbag and blew upward at a strand of hair falling on her forehead.

"Hi, Nance." He paused, eyed her. "Everything all right?"

"Yeah … sure." But Roland wasn't convinced.

They spent a few minutes awkwardly chit-chatting about the weather and Nancy's teaching plans. Before long, Roland, still puzzled, excused himself. "I better go do my work assignment."

"Right." She licked her lower lip. "Look, I'd … like to talk to you sometime next week … um, in private."

Roland's face apparently showed concern. Nancy continued, "Oh, nothing to worry about. Nothing's wrong. Well, at least … sorry, Roland, I can't talk straight. Can we figure out somewhere to meet where no one will bother us?"

"Yeah, I guess. I'll think about it and let you know."

"Thanks, and I will too. See ya later."

What on earth did Nancy have in mind? Surely nothing like … what he'd had with Barbara.

The rest of the day he racked his brain. Must be a pretty dark secret, surely connected to Barbara or maybe Albert. And how would Nancy know anything like that?

Unless she'd heard something from Will Sandberg.

An idea had been jelling, forming in his mind about a place to meet. Somewhere off the beaten path where they'd be alone.

He knew just the place.

CHAPTER 49

Roland
Tuesday

It was nine o'clock when Roland arrived at work. Charlie had told him to come in later until things returned to normal, assuming that would happen. No one around campus paid much attention to Roland these days, so he and Charlie remained guardedly optimistic.

"Morning, Roland." Charlie's perpetual cigarette dangled from the corner of his mouth. "Nice weather we're having. Say, I ran into Will Sandberg yesterday, and we were saying how things have simmered down around here. That you should be more comfortable. Hope you are, son."

"Yeah, I think so. Heard no remarks, and most kids stay out of my way. Almost avoid me like I'm contagious or something." Roland hung up his brown windbreaker and tugged at his shirt cuffs. Good to get rid of his parka for now anyway.

"Ya know, me and Sandberg thought it was a good sign for you, but maybe for the whole town too. We haven't heard much anti-Indian talk. Who knows, maybe folks have found other things to gripe about since the uproar has gone down some."

Roland hid a scoff. "Sure hope so, but…" He busied himself with straightening out the paper, pens, and other office items on the table. He knew people wouldn't suddenly cozy up with the

Indians. "Guess they aren't as angry now. Since the cops can't find any new suspects, maybe they think the whole thing really was an accident."

Charlie crushed his cigarette out in a tin ashtray on the table. "Not sure about that. I think they're still suspicious, but maybe it's dragging on so dang long they're bored with the whole thing. Not as exciting anymore."

"Right," Roland agreed and checked the assignment board as Charlie shuffled away. His boss's words about people being tired of Barbara's case had stung, although Charlie meant no offense.

The idea of the townsfolk getting bored and finding the case unexciting stuck in his craw. So that's what Barbara's life amounted to? A perp hadn't turned up, so they give up and find other stuff to keep 'em entertained? However, Roland would be off the hook if the case closed.

His pal, Larry, joined him at the table. "Howdy, Roland. Wanna head out and transport the extra chairs to the gym?"

"Number one on the board. Get it over with.".

He and Larry pushed their platform carts down the hall to retrieve the chairs.

"Haven't seen the cops nosing around for days now," Larry said. "Nothin' goin' on."

"What happens if they find nothing? I mean, like in months?" Roland asked. "Do they just keep at it or tuck it away in some forgotten file cabinet?"

"I think they'd call it a cold case then. Not sure, but yeah, they'd stuff the files away and maybe open them again someday. Don't seem right to just forget about her." Larry stopped to blow his nose with a red bandana.

"Yeah," Roland muttered. Of course, he couldn't react too strongly to Larry's words. Didn't want him to think Roland had known Barbara personally, or even known her at all.

Later, as he hauled endless folding chairs, lining up rows for graduation, Roland tried to think of other things. Like the past weekend at home on the reservation. His pa, in usual form, spewed plenty of opinions and advice for Roland. *Ya should've told yer boss you'd quit the job and get outta town far away. He'd understand. Don't need to listen to Moose all the time, ya know. He gets some highfalutin ideas in his head.*

Over the years, Roland had learned to go along with Pa's comments; easier than arguing or debating him. So, he'd changed the subject and told him and Dinah that he told Jasper the legend of the Wendigo. They laughed at Jasper almost tossing his cookies.

Back at the work area, the guys prepared for their lunch break. "Wanna come to the break room with us, Roland?" Larry asked.

"Some other time," Roland waved them ahead. Maybe one of these days he'd join in, but he still felt out of place, awkward at conversation with white guys.

•   •   •

At three o'clock, Roland had reached the parking lot when Nancy appeared like a ghost.

"God, where did you come from?" Roland nearly backed against the wall by the exit.

"Sorry," Nancy said. "To tell the truth, I was kinda lying in wait for you."

Roland smiled. "Yeah, bet I know why."

They slinked around a corner, trying to make themselves invisible. Roland lowered his voice. "I came up with a place to meet."

"Good," Nancy said. "I tried, but I couldn't think of anywhere."

"Well, I know a place. I kind of discovered it last fall. You know down by the lake, right on the shore there are some wooden benches...." Roland continued to describe the spot he had met Barbara a few times.

Nancy nodded. "Yeah, I can picture it. Never noticed the half-hidden spot, but sounds easy enough to find."

"Do you wanna meet on Friday? Charlie said I could leave early, slip out whenever I wanted."

Nancy paused. "Yeah, it'll have to be Friday. How about three-thirty?"

"Okay," Roland said. "Let's give each other about twenty minutes to wait in case something comes up."

"See ya then." Nancy turned to leave.

"Gotta confess, Nancy, you really have me guessing. I can't think of any secret you'd have to tell."

"I know, but I can't talk about it here; someone could come along any minute. Just a few more days to wait." She gave a curious smile and was on her way.

Roland crossed the parking lot to his car, more curious than ever. He couldn't shake the feeling that something would put the kibosh on their meeting. Something ominous floated in the air. But what?

CHAPTER 50

Nancy
Friday

At last, the day had come to show Roland the diary. I'd been dithering around, trying to hide my nerves from Peggy. After she left for work, I stayed put. My last two classes were this afternoon, so I strolled along by myself while butterflies flipped in my stomach. I loved the outdoors with warmer temperatures each day and the sparsely spattered snow. I breathed in the refreshing air and felt more relaxed.

My last class ended early, so I killed time in the library, attempting to find something to read or write. No use. I couldn't concentrate on anything except revealing Barbara's diary to Roland. Was I doing the right thing? How would he feel knowing she wrote about him?

When 3:30 crept closer, the butterflies danced, but with heavy feet. I assured myself if I had a last-minute change of heart, I could back out, tell Roland I thought it best to postpone the situation. Eventually, next month would come and go, and I would leave town after graduation. But how could I leave Roland in the lurch today? To be fair, I should consider him, not just me.

For the tenth time, I reached down and felt the small journal tucked safely inside my jacket pocket. The smooth vinyl edges of the cover would surely bend and become worn-looking from opening and closing it so often, along with my fondling its delicate texture.

The students had thinned out by now, anxious to escape campus for the weekend. Oh God, I was almost to the exit by the parking lot. Only a few more minutes.

Thankfully, the sun still bathed the sky with warm temperatures, so we could sit by the shore in comfort. The diary deserved our full attention.

I walked down the incline toward the lake, the ground hard, almost bare of snow. I basked in the scent of pine trees guarding the shores of Spirit Lake. I'd always loved the sight of decades-old three wooden benches about ten feet apart facing the waters. A part of campus landscape, familiar as an old painting.

I made my way past the last bench and found the pathway bend Roland had described. I kept on the path amongst several birch trees. I spotted him right away.

Roland sat unmoving on a lone bench, gazing at the shoreline and water beyond. He wore faded jeans and a tan windbreaker, the soft breeze fluttering his straight black hair.

"Roland," I called. "You made it."

"Yeah, got here early. Nothing like a lake to make you feel calm and let you think." He held his ski hat on his lap, folding and refolding it.

I sat beside him. "I haven't seen a soul since outside the parking lot door. Everyone's heading the other way."

We sat in awkward silence. "Well?" Roland asked.

"Well," I echoed. We both chuckled.

I shifted my back and gingerly reached into my pocket. I sensed Roland's eyes on my hand. "Let's get right to it." My hand trembled as I eased the diary out and held it on my lap.

I didn't want Roland to notice my hands shaking, but too late for that. He eyed the book.

"What's that?"

"A diary. A very special one. I want to explain why I have it and then … and then …" Crap, I was getting all jumbled up. "Anyway, Roland, you'll have to have patience, um, I'm sorry this isn't easier. If you'll just hear me out and then talk when I'm done, that'll be best."

"Okay." Roland's face was a blank slate.

"Well, a couple days before Barbara's funeral in Grand Rapids, I helped Judy and Doc Sandberg and a couple other family members pack up her dorm room. To cut a long story short, I discovered a …"

I went on to express why I kept the diary, although I really didn't exactly know. I told Roland it took me weeks to read the whole thing off and on.

I cleared my throat, realizing I was clutching the diary to my chest. "Well, um, I finally finished it." I looked up. Sweat beaded Roland's forehead.

"At the end, she wrote something." My words emerged slowly.

"Oh God, no." He wiped his face with the back of his hand.

"It'll be all right." I touched his arm. "But I want you to read it and keep it if you like."

"I don't know. Not sure I should read it or keep it. I … I need to think." He was obviously wary.

"I don't want you to be embarrassed. But I hoped it would make you feel like, well, honored and worthwhile. Of course, you're still in, um, mourning." Suddenly I felt intrusive; like I was spying on a past he wanted to keep private.

Roland eyed the diary, then looked up and contemplated the lake once more.

Abruptly, we both turned toward the western shores. "Roland, is that a loon?"

"I think so. Kinda early for them to be out, but sure sounds like it."

We both stood, craning our necks, taking several steps toward the warbling cry of the Minnesota state bird. Nothing to see. Perhaps we needed the distraction.

We sat back down. "One of my favorite sounds in the whole world," I said. "It's so beautiful in a melancholy way, like they're searching for something."

"Yeah, we can all understand that, I think." Roland's voice soft.

We sat silently for a second. He made no effort to take the diary.

"Clouding up a bit." Roland glanced at the sky. "Maybe we should—"

"Wait. You haven't looked at this yet." I held up Barbara's book.

"I don't know if I should. Or …" Roland squirmed.

"Should I just show you certain pages? Or at least the last few? And don't worry, I'll always keep it hidden. Nobody will ever see it."

Roland shrugged. "Okay, maybe the last couple pages."

I turned to the end and held the diary open for him to read. He took the book, holding it close to his face. "Kinda hard to read," he murmured.

"Yeah, the pages are small, and so is her handwriting. And some of the letters are loopy or something."

"Sorry, Nance, I learned handwriting in school, but I'm not used to reading it much anymore. Most things are printed or typed I guess."

He held the diary toward me and shrugged. Was he embarrassed? I couldn't tell.

"Do you mind if I just read certain parts to you? It won't take long."

"I suppose."

I heard uncertainty in his voice. I paused as I selected where to begin. "This is where it pertains to you, Roland. I haven't said it, but you know by now your name is in it. But a lot of the diary is Barbara's writing about classes, roommates, and all that."

I began reading aloud.

CHAPTER 51

Nancy

I felt Roland's black eyes glued on me. My voice quivered as Barbara's words came alive.

"I have so many feelings about us, but the truth is loving you is such sweet sorrow, which I borrowed from Romeo and Juliet except those lovers were parting. I feel both happy and tearful at the same time. And even if we can't end up together in years to come, I'm so thankful I found you and became a happy person. You said we were two lonely spirits who found each other. And I treasure the picture of the eagle taped on the next page. Someone in your family drew it."

I turned the page and showed Roland the pen and ink drawing of the majestic eagle perched on a lone tree branch.

"Oh, God," he choked. With trembling hands, he took the diary and held the pages against his chest. "My aunt Lulu drew lots of birds and animals. She gave that to me and … "

"That's really special," I said. "See the heart beside its beak? Obviously, Barbara drew it to add her feelings."

Roland sniffled, then nodded, handing the book back to me. "I can't bear to hear any more."

I pointed to her final words and read aloud. "I'll always love you, Roland."

He shook his head back and forth, back and forth, as he watched the lake. We sat in melancholy silence, only the trees hearing our thoughts.

Roland spoke. "I need to tell you that … that Barbara was really important to me. She was the only one I could talk to, and she wanted to hear about the Indian way of life, my family. We were two lost souls who met each other."

He hesitated. "But I knew she fell in love with me, well, you can tell by her diary. But I'm sorry, I just … just loved her like a sister or a friend, even though we kissed a couple times. She was younger, like my kid sister. Of course, because of me being an Indian, we could never be a couple. I know it happens, but I think it's against the law. Anyway, it's unheard of except maybe in olden times."

"Yes, I understand, Roland. But I guess I thought, or … I don't know what I thought. I felt the connection was good for both of you, and —"

"Oh, yes, it was. But I knew nothing good would come in the end, and to tell you the truth, I was getting ready to kind of back away. I mean, not like a real break up, but I hoped to meet less and less. Best for her to find friends who were like her."

"Maybe so," I said, but for some reason I was disappointed he didn't share Barbara's feelings for him. I must be a romantic. The intrigue of forbidden love or something like that.

In unspoken agreement, we gathered our jackets and bags, knowing it was time to depart. Still holding the diary I'd planned to give to Roland, I lifted it and said, "Would you —?"

Roland slowly shook his head. "It's not for me, Nance. It's for you to decide."

A lump grew in my throat, and I gently returned Barbara's hopes and dreams to my pocket.

. . .

Tomorrow I'd be busy packing all day for my new life of student teaching. Then graduation.

I wondered if our meeting at the lakeshore would be the last time I'd ever see Roland Nightbird.

CHAPTER 52

Roland
Tuesday

The air was crisp and clear, the sun poking itself through giant Norway pines as Roland drove along the lakeside road to campus. Still in shock from his meeting with Nancy, he tried to let the whole revelation of the diary sink in. Feeling more apprehensive than usual about showing up for work, he recalled Nancy's promise to always keep it hidden. He needed to quit worrying needlessly and act normal.

Coaxing himself to think of other things, he parked his car and made his way into the building. He recalled how he'd spiritually felt one with the earth after his weekend on the reservation with family. He and his pa had hunted the marshlands for pheasants, listening to red-winged blackbirds and chickadees sing their melodies.

His sister, Bonnie Sue, was home for a short visit. With her long, shiny black hair, infectious wide grin, and perky disposition, she always lit up the place. *Staying outta trouble, big bro? Don't wanna laugh too hard!* She was the only one who could joke with him about serious matters. And he sure needed humor these days. He and pa didn't laugh much; not like they used to.

Will Sandberg's cheerful voice interrupted his musings. "Good morning, Roland." They stood in the hallway near Roland's work area. "It's been a while since I've seen you."

"Yes," Roland said. "Nothing much happening." He thought of the secret he must keep.

"No news from the police." Sandberg waited a beat. "I don't know how you'd feel, but I've heard some talk about the case being closed due to lack of evidence."

"I'd be relieved that maybe I can go forward, but people still won't forget that I was under suspicion." Roland sensed glances from a few students who ambled by.

"What bothers me." Sandberg softened his voice. "Is Barbara won't get justice unless there's new evidence from the doctors that it was an accident. But that's doubtful."

"I agree." Roland lowered his head.

"Well, take care of yourself, son," Sandberg said. "I'd like to chat again sometime about other things. I always enjoyed hearing about your family and your Chippewa culture."

"Yes, sir, we'll do that." Roland gave a half wave as they turned to go their separate ways.

After Roland reached his workspace, Charlie strolled in, the ever-present Chesterfield drooping from his mouth. "Howdy, Roland. What's new?"

"Nothing, boss, and that's a good thing." Roland stepped toward the assignment list.

"Go ahead with inventory," Charlie said. "Give you some peace and quiet till Larry and them haul their butts in." He slogged away, pant cuffs dragging on the floor.

Working alone allowed Roland to let his guard down. Not worry about saying the wrong thing. Jasper was the only person he could talk freely to. But of course, there had been Barbara. Poor kid. He had even considered speaking to his grandma Dinah for spiritual strength. She'd always told her family to seek the woods and lakes; that each tree, flower, bird or beast was a spirit that would be a refuge in times of trouble. But he had chickened out on speaking to her.

An hour later, his task complete, Roland shuffled back to his workplace to join the crew and work until lunch break.

•   •   •

It was early afternoon when Roland heard the news. Charlie surreptitiously took him aside and sidled him into the office.

Charlie closed the door and sat at his desk. "Have a seat, kid. Just want you to know, that they've dropped the case."

"What?" Roland sank into a chair.

"Got a call from the cops that they're closing the case for now. They've been spinning their wheels, coming up with no evidence. Said they talked to the county judge and he's a hardnose on following the letter of the law. Just hearsay, no hard evidence, no arrests."

"So ... so they're giving up? The killer or whoever caused the injuries goes free?"

"Guess so, kid." Charlie puffed his cigarette. "Doesn't seem right, but hate to say it, you and Melowski were the only two they could've charged. The one cop, Bergstrom, said there were other allegations he couldn't reveal, but nothing they could prove."

Roland sat, stunned, even though he'd heard the probability of closing the investigation. This was a real blow to Barbara's memory and her family.

"Does everyone know the news? College kids and townspeople?" Roland asked.

"Not sure. I talked to Sandberg after I heard, and he already knew." Charlie squashed his cigarette into the ashtray. "According to him, there won't be an official announcement or memo sent out. Knox doesn't want anyone to get riled up, wants to cover up negative stuff. He hopes people will gradually forget about the whole mess."

Roland wordlessly nodded.

Charlie stood. "I haven't told the guys around here, but they'll hear soon enough. Wanted you to know first."

"Thanks, boss." Roland headed for the door.

He forgot to ask Charlie if this would be considered a cold case that may be reopened someday, or was it over and done with?

Roland reminded himself to call Jasper tonight. He'd probably be relieved no one would end up arrested. Had to call Pa too. And there was Nancy. Had she heard the news? Since she was away teaching in Green Earth, someone would probably call her. Peggy, most likely.

Roland wished they could discuss the situation. Nancy had always been kind to him, especially lately. A smart, friendly girl like her, why didn't she have a boyfriend?

After graduation, she'd be gone for good. Too bad they couldn't meet at the lakeshore one last time. Or maybe they could.

CHAPTER 53

Nancy
Tuesday

My second day of student teaching had gone pretty well. I observed my supervising teacher, Mrs. Murphy, conduct her English classes. I would gradually ease myself into teaching four classes and a study hall. Even though I wasn't all that busy, I went home exhausted each day.

My roommate, Gail, and I had rented part of a duplex several blocks from Green Earth High School. She'd majored in math, and was smart, amiable, and easy to live with.

We lounged on a couch and armchair in the teeny living room.

"God it's so boring, sitting all day observing other teachers." Gail lit an Old Gold and inhaled deeply.

"I know." I puffed away on my Winston. "I was excited at first, but after half a day, the novelty wore off."

When the phone jangled, we both stared at it. "You wanna get it?" I asked.

"Nah, probably for you." Gail sipped her Pepsi and tapped the ash off her cigarette into a tin ashtray.

"May be Mom," I said. The long-distance rates went down after 7 p.m., so most folks waited till then to call.

I picked up the receiver and sat by a table lamp across the room. "Oh, hi, Peg. Is everything all right?"

Gail glanced at me as I continued. "Really? Damn, I wondered when it would happen. I'm gonna let Gail listen in."

I held the phone out so we could both hear. After greeting Gail, Peggy went on. "Yeah, the case is closed and will probably go cold. May never reopen. The whole campus was buzzing about it at quitting time."

"How did you all find out?" Gail asked. "An announcement?"

Peggy explained that the police had notified people on campus, but no official news on the radio or anything, nor a memo from Knox. "I heard there would be a blurb in the newspaper tonight or tomorrow. I don't get the paper, but someone at work will have it."

"It's sad in a way," Gail said. "Barbara is being forgotten so fast … other than her family and good friends."

"What does Judy say?" I asked. My cigarette had burned down to the filter.

"She says Dave is pretty upset his sister won't get justice. Not now anyway. He hadn't told the Gruens yet."

"I suppose Roland knows about it," I said.

"I'm sure he does. They would've told his boss, Charlie, and he probably told Roland." Peggy paused. "Well, this is costing me, so I better go. Just wanted you to know."

We said our goodbyes, and Gail and I continued conversing. Since I hadn't socialized with Gail much, I hadn't gaged her view on Indians, so I avoided the subject of Roland. It occurred to me that creep, Melowski, would be free to strut around as if nothing happened.

Ten minutes later, the phone rang again. "Good Lord, someone else calling about the investigation?" I answered the phone, and said, "Hi, Mom, I'll bet you're calling to tell me that Barbara's case is closed."

"Oh, you know already. Peggy or Judy must've called." Mom paused. "Your father heard about it at work, so he … well, you know. Word sure gets around."

"Yeah, and I don't want to imagine what he had to say. But we can talk more this weekend when I'm at Peggy's. We can meet somewhere." I didn't want to waste Mom's money on a phone call.

"Fine. I'll tell you about it when we meet. Say hi to Pete and Robin, and I'll see you soon." I stifled a yawn.

"I love you, Nancy. You take care of —"

"I will. Good night."

"What about —"

"Bye, Mom."

I joined Gail on the couch. "Talk about the Minnesota goodbye." I'd heard the expression all my life, usually referring to women whose farewells were endless.

She laughed. "Same way with my mom."

• • •

Later, lying in bed, thoughts of Roland stuck in my mind. I confessed that lately, I'd thought if he were white, or even if I were Indian, I'd be interested in dating him. But like Barbara, I knew that could never happen. I hadn't heard of anyone marrying outside their race. Well, there was Lucille Ball and Desi Arnaz. But that seemed different. Maybe because they were celebrities.

Even Catholics and Protestants didn't marry one another. Mom would faint if I ever brought a Catholic guy home just to introduce.

I truly hoped to meet Roland again before I ditched Eklund for good.

CHAPTER 54

Roland
Friday . . . Several weeks later

The minute he walked into Main Hall for work, Roland sensed something in the air. Tension he could slice. No one looked at him. Students lowered their voices. Hushed conversations.

Something big had happened. Shuffling down the hallway, Roland lowered his head, eyes darting back and forth. By the time he reached the work area, his heart was ramming against his rib cage. He hung his jacket on the rack and stashed his old metal lunch bucket in his cabinet.

"Hi, Roland," Charlie said as he walked in the room. His voice sounded tight, lower than usual.

"Mornin'," Roland said, waiting for the ax to fall.

"Let's go have a seat." Charlie waved toward his office.

Roland stumbled over the chair leg as he sank down.

"Got some bad news, son." Charlie took a drag on his Chesterfield. "A couple days ago, Albert Melowski was in a car accident. Pretty bad. It's touch and go if he'll make it."

"Really? What happened?" Roland couldn't stop his right eye from twitching.

"Al had been to a party at a cabin across the lake. Guess he got pretty loaded and left by himself. Roads were clear, but you know, winding and narrow. He must've been speeding 'cuz he missed a curve and lurched straight into the woods, crashed head on into a huge tree trunk."

Charlie relayed more details: no one found him for at least an hour, nobody around to hear the crash, he may be transferred to Duluth or Minneapolis for head injury, had a back injury too.

Roland narrowed his eyes as he listened. "So, he might not make it?"

Charlie shook his head. "They're not saying much, but no, he may not. Haven't heard the odds yet."

Neither man spoke for a minute. "Don't know what to say," Roland stammered. "I mean, um, I don't know. I suppose people wish it was me, not Albert."

Charlie pointed a stern finger at Roland. "Don't even think that. The guy was drunk. Everybody knew he drank like a fish." He fiddled with his rumpled shirt sleeve. "In fact, between you and me and the gate post, Al did this to himself. His own fault." He leaned forward, lowered his voice. "But I never said that."

Roland nodded, but hesitated to respond. He wanted to say that maybe if Al dies, Barbara will get the justice she deserves. Of course, he would not express that opinion out loud to anyone. Except maybe Nancy.

•　•　•

Back at his work table, Roland knew he wouldn't get much done. Maybe Al would die as punishment for what he did. Truth be told, Roland hoped so. So, when would all this end? Maybe he should've taken off for South Dakota when Pa told him to.

Larry and the crew scurried in one by one, all chattering non-stop about Albert.

"I heard Al's old man is raising hell with the college big shots," Larry said, sitting beside Roland. "Wants to sue everyone in sight, like the kid's folks who own the cabin, the store where they bought booze, and God knows what else."

Roland scoffed, but tried to act his usual reserved self. "That's something," he said.

Curt chimed in. "Like those jackass kids don't show fake IDs in liquor stores, or sneak it from their folks."

"Heard much about Melowski's girlfriend? How's she taking it?" someone else asked.

Roland listened with half an ear as they droned on. He'd had enough. He pretended to need the bathroom and left.

He thought of Nancy. She must know the news. Someone would've called her in Green Earth. She probably felt the same way as him about justice for Barbara. Albert getting his just desserts, or whatever the saying was.

He'd try and run into Nancy on graduation weekend and hopefully make a plan to meet at the lake. On Friday, the seniors would gather at the college for cap and gown fitting, not a formal event. The ceremony was scheduled for Sunday. Roland would work all weekend, so surely, he'd see Nancy.

Wouldn't he?

CHAPTER 55

Nancy
Friday before graduation

Boisterous chatter and carefree laughter filled the gymnasium of a hundred students swirling together, trying on caps and gowns for Sunday's ceremony. Everything felt surreal. I'd finally reached the big weekend: graduation, the day I'd been waiting for.

I'd finished student teaching, and for the first time in my life, I'd succeeded at something. At least, according to my supervisors. Sure, plenty of challenges presented themselves, like two unruly boys getting into a fist fight right in the middle of *Our Town*. But I'd survived. Can't say the same for them.

As for Albert Melowski, I didn't shed a tear over him. He was hospitalized in Duluth, having undergone two back surgeries. The docs didn't know if he'd walk again. A tragedy for anyone else. My opinion? He had it coming, but I'd wanted him to suffer more, like in a court of law. But, maybe it's worse to be paralyzed, so I guess Barbara got the justice her family had sought.

"Nancy!" Judy dashed toward me, wearing a cotton skirt and saddle shoes, hair in a pony tail. "Have you been fitted yet?"

"No, on my way to the table now. Sure is crowded." I straightened the neck scarf around my blouse. "It's almost hot out."

Dave Gruen joined them. "Too bad it's supposed to rain on Sunday. We may end up in the gym instead of the stadium." He put an arm around Judy. A difficult day for Dave; an empty seat next to his parents.

They meandered toward the side, away from the mainstream. "Judy, what's it like to have Loreen home again?" I asked.

Judy scoffed. "Mom's not back for good yet. After graduation, she'll probably go back to Chicago until she and Dad come to an agreement or whatever. Mom's bigotry is still a sore point. Don't know if Dad can live with that or if she'll change."

I shrugged. I knew that particular leopard wouldn't change her spots. "I'm sure I'll see her Sunday after all the pomp and circumstance. Anything new on the wedding?"

Dave gave Judy a peck on the cheek and disappeared into the throng.

"We're pretty sure it'll be the end of August. I hope you'll be here as my maid of honor."

"We'll have to see. I'm hoping one of my applications for California will turn out." I had mixed feelings about the wedding. I didn't want to be stuck in Eklund if California came calling.

"Well," Judy shrugged. "Peg and my other friends will be here, but I'd rather ..."

I noted the line at my assigned table was thinning out, so I told Judy I'd see her later. I threaded my way over to wait my turn.

Afterwards, cap and gown in hand, I wandered up and down the hallways hoping to spot Roland. Ready to give up after ten minutes, I caught sight of him pushing a platform cart stacked with cardboard boxes. I scampered up behind him. "Gotta minute?"

Startled, he turned. "Oh, Nance, it's you." He eyed our surroundings, but the few kids in sight seemed wrapped up in their own business.

"I'll just take a second. I'm free tomorrow afternoon around two-thirty or three. I'd … I'd really like to meet at the lake, same place as before. What do you think?"

He gave me a warm smile. "Yeah, I'd like that. Lots to catch up on. Let's shoot for two-thirty."

"Great. Glad I ran into you, Roland. See you tomorrow."

On my way out, I figured, no, hoped, he may have been hanging around the gym area wishing he'd run into me.

Our main subject of conversation would be Barbara, but I was curious if he'd heard the latest on Albert's accident. According to the rumor mill, there may have been another car involved.

Someone who wanted Albert out of the picture?

CHAPTER 56

Nancy
Saturday

Another bright, periwinkle sky smiled on me. Perfect for sitting at the lakeshore with a friend. Yes, I considered Roland my friend.

I was finishing my lunch with Mom, Robin, and Pete. Dad was conveniently absent; said he had work to do at the station. Since I was living at home again after student teaching, the atmosphere was understandably tense, awkward. I'd been able to shake away some dire memories of Dad's cruelty, but we'd barely spoken since I arrived two days ago.

"I think the war hollowed out the goodness in him," Mom had said recently. "Yes, Nancy, he was a good person before Bataan. Well, not perfect, but who is?"

"I know, Mom. Maybe someday we can forgive each other." I doubted that, but I couldn't carry the burden of anger for the rest of my life.

I helped clear the table and rinsed off plates crusted with leftover tuna hotdish.

"What if it rains tomorrow, Nance?" Pete asked. My kid brother was growing up; I detected the shadow of a mustache on his round, freckled face.

"We'll all sit in the gym, stupid," Robin said. "You've heard that ten times already."

"Have not," he pouted and left the room.

I looked at Mom. "I'm gonna miss this, the sound of bickering and—"

"No you won't, ya lucky stiff. Wish I could go to California." Robin twisted the end of her golden pony tail.

I felt a trace of sadness. "When I land a job, you can visit me, if you stay out of trouble here at home."

"Very funny."

Later, on my way out I gave Mom an extra-long hug.

•   •   •

Ten minutes later, I walked down the grassy incline to the lake and wondered when I'd ever return to the sandy shore-lined charm of Spirit Lake. I breathed in the nostalgic scent of pines and water as I listened to the lilting harmony of birdcalls. I made my way to the partly hidden bench and brushed twigs and leaves off the splintered wood before I sat.

Bending forward to roll up the cuffs of my pedal pushers, I noticed a sizeable black smudge on my right saddle shoe. "Damn," I said aloud. "I just polished these."

"Must be very irritating."

I jolted up at the husky voice. "Shit, Roland. You about gave me a heart attack."

He gave a throaty laugh. "Sorry. Couldn't resist it." Roland's red checked shirt and crisp jeans made him look spiffy, but I didn't dare tell him. He'd feel embarrassed.

Roland settled himself on the bench, and we sat taking in the lake scene.

"I can hear the waves lapping on the shore," I said. "I suppose Thunder Lake is like this one, I mean the size."

"Actually, it's much bigger. Good that we both grew up by a lake."

I didn't want to waste time with small talk, so I dove right in. "Um, about Albert, have you heard the latest on his accident?"

"I think so. Charlie mentions it now and then." Roland seemed hesitant.

"According to the grapevine from yesterday, there's been some speculation. Don't ask me where it came from, but Peggy said there may have been another car at the scene. Someone noticed more tire markings where Al went off the road. They also saw some paint chips, just a few that were embedded somehow into the gravel." I peered sideways at Roland.

He frowned. "Hmm. I'm surprised. It's been how many weeks? How could tire tracks and paint still be there?"

"Good question," I said. "I asked Peg, and she didn't know. She'd heard that someone was nosing around there and called the cops to report what he saw. All very vague. But maybe someone hit Al from behind and forced him off the road."

Roland coughed. "If he was really drunk, that would make sense he'd miss the curve, like the cops thought."

"Yeah, they'll probably forget the whole thing unless ..."

"Unless Albert ends up dying." Roland finished my thought.

"God knows, there are plenty of people who'd like to see the guy get payback for what he did to Barbara." Like Roland, but how would he have known exactly where Al was that night?

"Yeah." Roland frowned. "But in the end, like my grandma's said many times, even if people get away with wrongdoing on earth, they'll be rightly judged in the spirit world."

I nodded. "That's a good belief." I wondered if Roland believed it himself. Time to change the subject.

I reached in my purse and felt the diary tucked in the bottom. I eased it out and held it. "I know you weren't sure if you —"

"No, Nancy. It belongs to you. Even though Barbara didn't realize it, you cared deeply about her. I think through her diary, you developed a special appreciation of who she really was." Roland sighed.

"I agree. She had a lot of depth for someone her age. Her problems with shyness would've vanished eventually." I waited a beat. "Judy said the Gruens are planning a memorial scholarship."

"Good. A perfect way for her name to live on."

I opened the diary to a page at the end. "I know it's painful, but I just wanted to read this sentence again."

"And even if we can't end up together in years to come, I'm so thankful I found you and became a happy person."

Roland sniffled noisily. "I'm … I'm a better person too."

I closed the book and put it away. Maybe I'd keep it close at hand forever. Too many emotions to sort out now.

"You know, whenever I'm around trees or woods, Longfellow's words go through my head." I waited.

"What are they? I wouldn't mind hearing if it's not too long."

I laughed. "Don't worry, take a few seconds." I began:

"This is the forest primeval. The murmuring pines and the hemlocks, Bearded with moss, and in garments green, indistinct in the twilight…"

"That's all I remember."

"Say it again." Roland stared ahead.

I repeated the lines, and then asked, "You must like it."

"Yeah, it reminds me of poems and sayings I've heard growing up. Like our beliefs, nature is part of me, speaks to me." Roland hesitated. "Jeez, I never talk like this."

"I love nature too," I added lamely. I wanted him to keep talking.

"Hey, are those loons out there?" Roland stood, peering at the lake shimmering in the sunlight.

I squinted and shaded my eyes. There they were, the telltale white spots on black feathers. "Listen to their wistful cries. I love the sound of their music."

We crept closer to the gravely beach. "Do you see two of them?" Roland pointed. "There they are, hard to see. They keep ducking under."

I wished I could bottle the peace and contentment that swept through me at this moment. Maybe this was one of those lifelong moments you always remember. Perhaps my heart's treasury would hold the safe kept memory of a lovely thing, or something like that. I forgot where those words came from.

We sat again, and I reluctantly checked my watch. "I suppose I should be going. And you must have to get back to work?"

"Charlie said I could leave early, so I'll probably head for Moose's place." Roland seemed in no hurry.

"Before we go, you'd said something about poems from your childhood. Do you know any of them?" I wanted to delay leaving.

Roland swept his burnished black hair from his forehead. "Not a whole thing, but a few words here and there."

"I'd like to hear them, that is if you're not scared," I teased.

He chuckled. "Maybe a little, but here goes:

"There, above in that cloudless sky, eagles fly…, like the peoples spirit and strength … There, in my dream, I am one with my ancestors, The only sound is the wind that moves the fluttering feathers."

"Oh my God, I love it. What a beautiful passage. Where is it from?" I marveled at how Roland's deep, smooth voice brought the poem to life.

"I have no idea who wrote it. I just heard it all the time. There's more to it, but I can't remember."

"I must say, you sounded like a real poet."

Did Roland blush? Hard to tell.

"This is turning into the Minnesota goodbye that I accuse my mom of doing all the time."

Roland chuckled. "My grandma is guilty of that too."

I gathered my purse and stood. "I guess the one loose end is Al's accident, and whether he was alone at the time."

"Yeah, and whether he'll live or ..." Roland stood beside me. "I still feel lousy about backing off from Barbara's ... our friendship."

"Oh Roland, I wish you didn't feel that way, but you knew what would be best for her. That's how much you loved her. Yes, love. A special love. Not romantic, but ... but ..."

We walked by the waters and around birches and pines toward Main Hall. This would most likely be the last time Roland and I would make this trek together.

After a minute, I stopped and touched his arm. "One more quote. I want you to really listen to these words from William Wordsworth, because they describe Barbara's gift to you."

"She gave me eyes, she gave me ears;
And humble cares, and delicate fears;
A heart, the fountain of sweet tears;
And love, and thought, and joy."

Then with a heavy heart, I said goodbye to Roland Nightbird.

EPILOGUE

One year later

Barbara Gruen's legacy lives on through a college scholarship for students majoring in English. Her parents continue to live in Grand Rapids, where both volunteer at a grief support center.

Dave Gruen married **Judy Sandberg** last August and they now live in Minneapolis. He teaches high school science and coaches basketball. Judy is a fifth-grade teacher at a nearby elementary school.

Peggy Olsen enrolled at Eklund State as a freshman in September. She qualified for a grant to help expenses and continues to work part-time in the admissions office. She sees a counselor twice a month to help her cope with lingering psychological problems.

Loreen Sandberg moved back to Eklund after living in Chicago for five months. She and **Will** agreed to give their marriage a second chance. Soldier has been happier ever since. Arriving in time for Judy's wedding, Loreen enjoyed advising her daughter on a proper wedding worthy of their social status.

Albert Melowski remains wheelchair bound after physical therapy and surgery proved unsuccessful. He lives in Crookston, Minnesota with his parents, who employ a full-time caretaker for him. He rarely has visitors, except last February on the first anniversary of Barbara's death when his old pal, **Earl Krepp** stopped in. He told Al he has no sympathy for him, only anger, and no regrets about the night of the accident. He never saw Al again.

Roland Nightbird moved to South Dakota last July. Although his job environment had become more promising, he decided he needed a change, and he now lives in Aberdeen with relatives. Since landing a maintenance job at a junior high school, Roland had found contentment. Dinah, his grandmother, died several months ago, but he couldn't make the funeral. **Uncle Moose** is keeping well and urges Roland to come home. Roland stays in touch with **Charlie** and **Jasper** through letters, which Charlie encouraged him to write. He mapped out a college course plan for Roland, hoping for his return.

Nancy Borg's dream of teaching in California came true last August after Judy's wedding. She drove to San Diego with **her mom**, where she moved in with a cousin. She landed a position teaching high school English in Escondido and put her mom on a train back home. Her father, **Theo,** remains at home, fighting his own demons. Nancy visited campus one day before Christmas and surreptitiously sought out Charlie to ask after Roland. He said he exchanges letters with Roland, whose handwriting is improving, and hopes he'll return and begin college classes. Roland's pal, Jasper, is an assistant mechanic at the gas station and still lives with his mom, Elsie.

Nancy often thinks of Roland, and plans to dream up a reason to ask Charlie for his address. Perhaps she'll write to him someday.

ABOUT THE AUTHOR

Meg Lelvis grew up in northern Minnesota and taught English and psychology in Houston and Dallas. Her first novel, *Bailey's Law,* won the 2017 Maxy Award for Best Mystery. Meg's second *Bailey* novel, *Blind Eye,* was released in April 2018. It won Maxy Award's runner-up for Best Mystery in 2018.

A Letter from Munich was her third novel, which won the 2020 PenCraft 2nd Place Award for Historical War. Her fourth book, *Back of the Yard,* won Indie Author TX Project for Adult Fiction in 2021 and was a finalist in the Hawthorne Prize in 2022.

Meg resides in Orlando with her husband and their Pyrenees dog, Chloe.

OTHER TITLES BY MEG LELVIS

NOTE FROM MEG LELVIS

Word-of-mouth is crucial for any author to succeed. If you enjoyed *Frozen Girl of Spirit Lake*, please leave a review online—anywhere you are able. Even if it's just a sentence or two. It would make all the difference and would be very much appreciated.

Thanks!
Meg Lelvis